An Affair
and a Promise

Arlene Grace

Stely Publishing

A division of Stely LLC
© Copyright 2015 Arlene Grace

ISBN-13:9780991453443
ISBN-10: 0991453441

Author's photography by: Cari Baun
Library of Congress Cataloguing-in-Publications
Data has been applied for.

With much love

I dedicate this book to my friend Ebba.

You are stronger than you think.

Chapter 1

*J*ulie Turner looked at her watch nervously. She wondered how much longer her flight to San Diego, California, was going to take. Her plane had taken off from Raleigh, North Carolina, at seven-thirty that morning and she was anxious to just get off. She looked out the window, trying to figure out what state they might be flying over, but could see nothing but clouds. As the flight attendant walked by, she asked, "Miss, can you tell me how much longer we have in the air?"

"Oh, I'd say about another hour before we're on the ground."

"Thank you," she said as she sat back in her seat and looked at her watch again.

As Julie tried to relax in her seat, her mind raced. She kept asking herself all kinds of questions and doubting the decision she'd made to even take the trip. *Am I making a fool of myself? I'm probably making a fool of myself. He won't even be there. That was twenty years ago. A lot has happened since then. I'm in my mid-forties. Who am I kidding? He probably doesn't even remember me.*

As she sat there for the next hour, her mind began to wander back to the reason she was even on this flight. She'd made a promise with a young man to meet twenty years from tomorrow at a park on Coronado Island across the bridge from San Diego. She had fallen deeply in love, but she had been married at the time. Having felt the commitment to her husband, she had ended it. But before they parted each to their own separate lives, they promised one another they would meet again. They'd even joked and laughed, speculating on whether he would be bald and she would be fat! They were always able to make light of things and tease one another, something she wasn't ever able to do with her then-U.S. Marine husband.

Brian Turner was a jock in high school. He was six feet tall, had brown hair and brown eyes, and a killer smile. His muscles bulged from under his T-shirt sleeves. He was the captain of the football team and the catch of their class.

Julie Nelson was a straight-A student and captain of the debate team. She was also the student body president. Not exactly the pair anyone would imagine ever getting together. But Brian had eyes only for Julie. They met in their junior year when Brian's family had moved to La Jolla, California. His father was a Marine and had been transferred to the base at Camp Pendleton. He and his older brother Chuck were military brats. Chuck was five years older and had joined the Marines right out of high school, continuing a family tradition of service.

Brian's first week at this high school he'd been assigned a "buddy" to show him around and tell him the ins and outs of the school. It was his first time attending a school that wasn't on a military base. The counselors thought it would be a good idea to have Julie do the honors since she knew the school so well. On the Wednesday afternoon of the first week, Julie mentioned to Brian that she would be participating in a debate and he should come just to see what it was all about. He did. As he sat in the classroom and watched Julie take charge of the debate against an opposing school, he couldn't believe his eyes and ears. This timid young woman who could barely make eye contact with him was kicking the opposing team's proverbial butts, chewing them up and spitting them out with every argument. Her other teammates, all of whom were male, allowed her to take the lead. Brian was impressed. She really caught his eye. She wasn't really his type, a very studious-looking skinny brunette with deep blue eyes and glasses. She was the last female he would have ever thought he'd ever be attracted to. There were already cheerleaders and the types with the *reputations* passing him notes and making eyes his way. But from that moment when he saw Julie with that "take-charge" attitude, he knew she was something special.

Not having much time for nonsense, Julie pretty much ignored Brian for the rest of the year. When their senior year started, Brian asked her to the Homecoming dance and she accepted. Not having ever attended a formal dance before, her mom had encouraged her. "Go for the experience," she told her. Julie really had no interest in going, and had caved in to the pressure just to get her parents and friends off her back. Brian's choice for Homecoming was the talk of the school. He had broken the Hearts of all of the Homecoming Court and cheerleaders who were attending. His friends teased him as well, but he didn't care. He was going to get Julie to like him if it was the last thing he did.

Julie went shopping for a dress with her mom, and they settled on a long silver halter dress and matching shoes. "I don't want high heels, mom," she protested. "I won't be able to walk, much less dance. And I don't even know how to dance! What am I to do?" she squealed.

"You just watch what others are doing and do the same thing. Just listen to the beat of the music and you'll be fine," said her mom.

The football team won the game that afternoon, and Brian was there to pick her up for the dance at the high school gym right at seven. The dance was set to begin at eight, and he wanted to take her out to dinner first. Julie's dad answered the door and let Brian in. Julie walked down the stairs with mom in tow, camera in hand. Brian looked up the stairs as she came down toward him and his mouth dropped open. She looked so different!

Mom started to take pictures as Brian gave her a white orchid wrist corsage. She made them pose. Julie felt very awkward but complied. She figured the sooner she got that over with, the sooner she could leave. Ten minutes later, they were getting into his Mustang and headed to the restaurant. He had made reservations at a rooftop restaurant near the school for convenience and to hopefully get a look at the sunset.

"Wow, you look so pretty. I don't think I've ever seen you without your glasses."

"Thank you," she said as she felt her cheeks turn hot. "They are only reading glasses, but the top half is clear. I just think it's a nuisance taking them off and on all of the time. So I had them made that way. I put them on in the morning and I take them off after I'm done studying when I get home. I didn't think I'd be doing much reading tonight, so my mom insisted I leave them home. I'm really not very hungry. Do you think I could just have the house salad?"

"Sure," he said as the waitress approached the table. "One house salad, one cheeseburger and two cokes please," he said. "So, what are you studying all the time? Don't you ever just want to have fun? You can't go through your senior year and not have fun."

"I have fun. I study for my debates. Those are fun. I want to be an attorney someday. Winning debates is good practice for me. What are you going to do after we graduate? Do you know what you might want to do?

"I'm going into the Marines," said Brian without hesitation. "In fact, I'm going to pre-register in January. I'll be eighteen then. I'll be a third-generation Marine. My grandfather was a Marine. My dad is a Marine and my brother Chuck is stationed on the East Coast. He loves the Corps. I can't wait!"

"Well, no wonder you don't have to give much thought to studying. You probably won't even take the SATs. You won't need those scores in the Corps."

"I guess you're right. We all have different callings. Are you putting me down?"

"Oh, I'm sorry Brian," she said with an embarrassed look on her face. "I didn't mean to hurt you at all. I'm just saying that it makes it easy knowing what you are going to do and focus on what's important to you. I'm looking forward to the dance," she said, trying to change the subject. "I've never been to a dance. I hope I don't embarrass you."

Brian looked at Julie with his crooked smile and big teeth. "You can't embarrass me. You're going to be the prettiest girl there."

Julie looked at the way Brian was staring at her. She never really hung out with boys but she did feel comfortable around him. It made her feel more at ease and she decided to just relax and have a good time. After all, she had a whole evening ahead of them.

When they got to the gym, the music was blasting so loudly they could hardly hear themselves talk. Brian led the way over to where the other jocks were hanging out with their dates to say hello. After a few minutes of everyone checking each other out, he asked Julie to dance. Off they went to the center of the dance floor. Brian was flinging his arms all over the place, so Julie decided to do the same. It was actually a lot of fun, and they spent the rest of the evening dancing nonstop. When the dance ended at eleven, Brian drove Julie home and walked her to the door. She felt awkward not knowing what to do next.

"I had a great time," she said looking down at her feet.

"Me too," said Brian. "Maybe we can take in a movie or something some other time."

"Oh sure," she said looking up and smiling. "That would be great. Well, good night and thanks again." She turned and stepped inside, not looking back. She let the door close behind her.

Her mom and dad were in the living room waiting up. "Well?" said her mom. "Did you kids have a good time?"

"Oh sure, it was fun. I'm really glad I went. He's really nice. We might go to a movie or something soon. Well, I'm going to bed, okay?" Julie waved at her parents and went upstairs to her room. Once inside, she hung her pretty dress in the closet and threw the shoes on the top shelf. She slipped between her covers. They felt cool and comfortable. As she snuggled and closed her eyes she began to think to herself that she really liked this young man. He was different from most of the others. He was funny and easy to be around. She rolled over, took a deep breath, and closed her eyes. She was asleep in no time.

Chapter 2

August 1982

*J*ulie and Brian dated the rest of the senior year and had become great friends. He was always good company but Brian wanted more. The night before leaving to go into active duty, he took Julie to his parents' house and up to his room.

Brian had kissed Julie before, but she had never let him do any touching or petting. That night while sitting on his bed, Brian told Julie that he loved her and wanted to marry her. Brian began to cry and told Julie that she needed to commit to him before he left and that he wanted to have sex. Julie felt sorry for Brian. He was so emotional she didn't know what to do. He wouldn't stop crying. So she gave in. Brian began to touch Julie's breasts and unbuttoned her blouse. She didn't do anything to stop him like she had the many times he had tried this before. He stood her up in front of him and undressed her. Julie wanted to die of embarrassment. She had never been naked in front of a boy before. Tears began to well up in her eyes and creep down her face. As he stood in front of her and dropped his pants. She looked the other way. It was very awkward for her. He placed Julie on his bed and laid on top of her. He kissed her lips while squeezing her breasts. It didn't feel good at all. He was squeezing too hard. She wasn't an expert but she knew he couldn't possibly know what he was doing. This didn't feel right at all. Before she knew it, he had plunged and entered her. She felt herself rip. There had been no attempt to lubricate her and was she was very dry and in terrible pain. She tried to complain and move out from under him, but he understood her squirming as if she was liking it and began to pound her, hard. Brian was a big guy and she couldn't move. She just laid there and focused on the ceiling light fixture and prayed it would be over with quickly. And it was. But now he had made a mess and was still laying on her with his dead weight.

"Get off of me!" she complained. "I can't breathe!" she yelled.

"Sorry baby, it was just so good. I lost control. I love you baby, I love you so much!" he said as he rolled off of her onto his side, very out of breath.

"I need to wash up. Where are my clothes?" She rolled off the side of the bed and gathered her things. Luckily, his parents weren't home. She ran to the hall bath and shut the door. The tears were streaming down her face. She was sobbing but was trying not to make any noise. The pain was terrible. It felt like she had been ripped apart. Julie sat on the toilet with wet paper to try to wipe him off of her, then she noticed blood. That made her cry even harder. This wasn't the way she had pictured losing her virginity. But it was gone and there was nothing she could do about it.

Brian drove Julie home and she didn't say a word. When he walked around to let her out of the car, he kissed her and told her his father was going to drive him in to catch the bus to the base at five in the morning and that he would write. Julie managed to mouth the words good-bye, and she walked in the house. She slammed the door and ran up to her room.

Basic training for a Marine was twelve weeks. She knew at least she would have that long to think about what had just happened. Did she love this boy enough to marry him? Is this all there was to sex? If it was, she didn't really see the big deal. It hadn't been pleasant enough to want to do it again. And what if she were to get pregnant? He had been in such a hurry he hadn't even used any protection.

Julie didn't sleep that night. She thought about everything that had just happened and decided to pray for the best and try not to think about it. School was starting for her in a week and she was grateful to have her studies to worry about.

As valedictorian, Julie had earned a free ride to University of Southern California. It was a three-hour drive from her home to the university. Her parents had saved for years to pay for her education. She was an only child and they had always wanted the best education for her. Her mom was a registered nurse and her dad was an engineer. But now that her studies were taken care of, they were able to pay for her to stay on campus in a dorm. Their finances would go a long way and take care of her law school education, as well.

Chapter 3

The last week in August and one week after her eighteenth birthday, Julie's mom and dad drove to Los Angeles in a van they had rented that was full of Julie's stuff she was taking into her dorm room. Julie followed in her new car. She'd decided to pledge to a sorority, but not until the following year. She really wasn't sure about that whole thing since she wasn't really a party girl, and wanted to check them out before making any commitments. Her mom was a Theta and was trying to persuade her in that direction. But Julie's goal was to finish getting her bachelor's in criminal law in three years. She had taken many of the basics already, and had been allowed to do so because of her GPA as well as her amazing SAT scores. That put her one step ahead of many of her classmates. Her full load would keep her busy and without much time for all of the nonsense that seemed to be part within the Greek system.

When they arrived, they made their way to the dorm room Julie had been assigned in June when they had been on campus for a "meet and greet." She was to share the room with another student who hadn't arrived yet. Julie decided it would be first-come, first-serve and chose the bed nearest the window. She had a thing for looking at the night sky to look for falling stars. While they were wrapping things up and discussing grabbing a bite before heading back home, the door flung open.

"Hey y'all! I'm TJ Miller. TJ is short for Teresa Jane, but y'all can call me TJ for short."

But short she wasn't! She stood about five feet, ten or eleven inches tall and had long curly fiery red hair. She had a big smile and a small slit between her two front teeth with cute freckles on her nose and cheeks. TJ walked over to Julie and shook hands and said, "You must be Julie. I've been looking forward to meeting you. I guess I missed you when we came to see the place. My mama and I came the week before y'all. I'm from Raleigh, North Carolina. You're a local gal, no?"

"Actually, we are from La Jolla, down south before you get to San Diego," said Julie's mom. "We hope you'll visit with Julie when you can. We'd love having you."

"Why thank you. I'm a Southern girl too, but from the *real* South. My mama is worried I might get in with the wrong crowd and all being this is California. But y'all seem nice enough. I hear you and I got the same scores on our SATs, Julie. I'm glad they didn't stick me in a room with one of those airheads, if you catch my meanin'. It'll be nice to have someone to talk to with the same goals as me. I'm going to law school. My daddy and my big brother Jake are attorneys in Raleigh and I'm going into the family practice. I'm the youngest of five and the only girl. Do you have any siblings?" she asked as she threw her suitcase on the bed.

"No, I'm it. I guess I fussed so much as a baby my parents didn't think they wanted to repeat that again and after they had me." They all laughed. "We were just going out to get a bite. Would you like to join us?" asked Julie.

"I'd really love to, but there is a couple of guys downstairs unloading a small truck with my stuff, and I'd better get unpacked. They are going to haul it up here any minute. Looks like y'all did that already. You go on ahead. It was really great meeting you folks. Promise not to lead your baby astray or anything like that."

Mr. and Mrs. Nelson waved as they stepped out the door with Julie. "She seems like she's nice enough," said Mr. Nelson.

"I hope she doesn't snore," said Julie, and they laughed and got in the car. They drove down the streets outside of the campus and found a small Mexican restaurant. Julie was there only in spirit. She was anxious to have her parents leave and get back to the dorm. She was looking forward to being on her own and to getting on with her life. She loved her folks and knew they had sacrificed a lot for her and her education, but it was time, and she was ready. Now it was her turn to make her dreams and her goals a reality. She knew if she were to succeed and become a good attorney, she could repay them in their later years.

Julie made her mom stop at a small grocery store on her way back to the dorm. She bought a chocolate cake and some ice cream to take back and share with her new roommate. She thought it would be a good ice breaker. When she got there, TJ was on the phone with her parents. When she saw the cake she said to her mom, "Gotta go! My new bestie just walked in with my crack!"

Julie was taken back with that remark. TJ ran toward her, took the cake to the small kitchenette counter they had and gave Julie a big hug. "*Girl*, you don't know how addicted I am to chocolate cake! Did they tell you this at the meet and greet?" She gave Julie a hug and said, "You and I are going to get along just fine! Let's cut this puppy up and do some damage."

Julie laughed as she saw TJ tearing into the cake. She cut Julie a small piece, and cut herself a whole quarter of the cake. "Sit, let's talk and get to know each other. You tell me your secrets and I'll tell you all about Jack Danger. He's my man!"

They sat and talked and laughed for what seemed hours. TJ seemed a bit uninhibited for a proper Southern girl. She told Julie that her family came from old money, and Jack Danger was from *new money*. He was the son of a family that owned a chain of tire stores in North and South Carolina that apparently did very well. Being from a family of highly educated people (mostly lawyers and judges), her daddy just didn't approve, but her mama thought "he was hot!"

TJ went into great detail about the romance between her and Jack Danger. Is seems they'd been going at it like dogs in heat since the beginning of their senior year. It fascinated Julie to hear all the details she was sharing, and seemed pretty experienced at sex for someone so young. Julie wasn't quite sure how she did it, but TJ got her to share her disastrous first and only experience at love making. She felt very comfortable talking to TJ, and knew they would become good friends. TJ reassured Julie that the first time wasn't usually the most pleasant experience for anyone, but told her to try to relax the next time, and just let it happen. She gave her some pointers on how to get Brian to slow down and take his time to make sure she was ready before plunging in. "Y'all will love it girl, you'll see. Have a couple of beers and tell him what you want and just let loose and have fun!" she told Julie.

Before they knew it, the cake was gone and so was the ice cream. Julie loved to hear her new friend talk about her home and North Carolina. She'd never been out of California before. TJ had a slight Southern drawl that Julie found interesting and very cute. She knew TJ was going to be very popular. She was the perfect combination of beautiful, smart, and cute. She was also very well-traveled. Her family obviously had taken their children all over the world. Julie envied that of her friend. She had always wanted to travel. That was one of her goals when she graduated from law school. But she had to graduate first.

Now, she had to concentrate on the weeks ahead. School was starting in two days. Tomorrow, they had to go to the book store, pick up their books, and make sure all of their classes were right. It appeared they were going to share some of their classes, and they were glad to be able to have a study partner built right in. Exhausted, they finally turned out the light at about one in the morning. When they'd settled in, TJ said to Julie, "Y'all don't snore do you?" They both giggled.

Chapter 4

The first semester flew by. Julie found out that TJ was a beast with her studies. She couldn't believe she had actually found someone as dedicated to her studies as she was. But that didn't mean she wasn't going to let this time of their lives go by without having a little fun and getting into a little trouble. TJ insisted they join in some of the toga parties and raids their friends invited them to. Julie thought TJ was a maniac at drinking beer. It seemed unnatural that anyone could consume that much brew one night and score a perfect grade the next day on chemistry test. It was something she'd become used to in high school when she went to parties with Jack. Her parents had never found out though. If they had, they wouldn't have let her out of the house again. Her grand-daddy was a hanging judge in Raleigh, and he would have made sure that Jack would have hung all right. As far as they knew, she was the perfect Southern lady, and Jack Danger was "the nicest young man."

Julie received letters from Brian almost weekly. He was upset because she hadn't been writing back as much as he would have liked. She blamed her heavy class load. She did miss Brian. They had always had a good time together and she was realizing now that she really did have feelings for him that she hadn't really dwelled much on before he left for Marine training camp. She was looking forward to seeing him when he came home after boot camp. They were hoping he would be home for Thanksgiving, but they weren't sure how much time he would have off after training before he was given his assignment.

On the third weekend in October, Julie had made plans to go home to La Jolla to spend her mom's birthday with her and her dad. It was really the first break she had given herself since getting to school. He parents were anxious to see her. Julie invited TJ to come along, but she declined. She claimed to have plans for that weekend. It seemed that Jack Danger was going to fly out to California for that weekend and they were going to lock themselves up in at a local motel. She was excited to see him and couldn't wait to pick him up at the airport.

Julie left school early that Friday afternoon, and after spending three and a half hours on the San Diego freeway, managed to get home in time for dinner. Her folks were delighted that she was home. She was glad to see them as well.

The next afternoon, Julie's dad gave her mom a barbecue and had invited mostly family and a few of their close friends. The weather was great. October was always warm and there was always that light fall breeze in the evenings. The family was glad to see Julie and she had to spend the afternoon answering questions about school and her plans for the future. Julie's mom was beaming with happiness to have her daughter home.

It was her fiftieth birthday. Julie helped light all the candles and passed cake out to everyone.

When everyone had left, Julie was in the kitchen. She had offered to clean up. She told her dad to go watch football and asked her mom to just sit. She was going to finish loading the dishwasher. Her mom sat on a stool at the breakfast bar, watching her daughter toil with delight.

"Well," she asked as she sipped her last glass of wine. "Have you heard much from Brian since he left? Has he called you?"

Julie knew this conversation was coming. She had been expecting it since she walked in the door. "Yes, he writes all the time and he's called a couple of times. They don't let him use the phone much, though. If he gets caught, they make him do like a couple of hundred pushups. So he just mostly writes."

"Have you two made any plans for the holidays? I mean, he'll probably be home for Thanksgiving, don't you think? I'm sure his parents are going to be glad to see him, too."

Julie didn't make eye contact with her mom, but she responded, "Right now we're just playing it by ear. He doesn't know if and when he'll get his orders. There is too much in question before we'll know for sure. But I'm sure we'll see each other at some point when he gets his leave."

That night when she went up to bed, she looked around her room. It all seemed foreign to her. Like she had lived there in some other lifetime. She was so focused on her future that this seemed to be very much in her past. But there was a sense of comfort, too. As she pulled the covers up, she turned the lights out and looked out the window to the side of her bed.

The stars looked so familiar to her. As if they had never moved. They were always in the same spot, more or less, since she was little. Looking at them was always something she enjoyed. She even talked to them when she was young and told them all of her dreams. She fell asleep many nights doing that.

In the morning, Julie's parents wanted to take her out to breakfast before she left to go back. She didn't want to get a late start. There was an exam Monday morning she had to study for and she also didn't want to get stuck in traffic. There was a football game at the Coliseum that afternoon, and she dreaded getting in the middle of it.

Early in the afternoon after a nice long breakfast, Julie hugged her parents and began the drive back to the university. She had been thinking about having to face Brian very soon. She was actually excited to see him and wanted very much to be with him again. In one of his letters to her, he had made it very clear that he couldn't wait to be with her, too. He had told Julie that he wanted nothing more than to make her his wife. Julie knew it was too early for them to do that. They were much too young. Her studies were her first priority. If he wasn't willing to wait for her to meet her goals, then as far as she was concerned, he could just go on his merry way. Brian knew they were too young, too. He was just very anxious to settle down. His parents had been married young and always thought he would also. But he knew if he wanted it to be Julie, he was going to have to wait.

Shortly before three in the afternoon, Julie pulled into her parking space by the dorm room. She grabbed her overnight bag out of her trunk and made her way up the stairs to her door. There was music blasting from the opened doors of several dorm rooms. It was loud in the corridor. Typical for a weekend.

Julie put her key in the door and opened it. What she saw made her freeze in her tracks. Kneeling on the floor at the foot of TJ's bed was a man wearing no shirt, with a huge back. He was sporting wing tattoos that spanned from the shoulders to his waist. He was wearing a pair of jeans. Wrapped around his head were two legs with red stilettos on the feet. Now, away from the noise in the corridor, Julie could clearly hear her roommate shouting, "Oh JD, yes JD do it, do it more! Don't stop! Don't stop!"

Julie didn't know what to do at that point, and was sure they had been too busy to notice she had even opened the door. So, she decided to just creep back out into the hall, and wait until the shouting stopped. After about fifteen minutes, she knocked on the door before entering. TJ answered, looking very disarrayed. "Oh, hi Sugah'! Come on in. I want you to meet Jack Danger!"

Jack extended his hand, and knowing where it had just been, Julie opted to just nod and say hi.

"I've heard so much about you I feel like I know you." Jack, who was now sitting on the end of TJ's bed, put his T-shirt back on and stood up, zipping his pants.

"He was just saying his good-byes!" said TJ with a kind of laugh. "I'm fixin' to take him to the airport and we had a few minutes to kill, so we were just gett'n some last minute huggin' and kissin' in."

"I hope you'll come to visit North Carolina real soon. I know everyone there is dying to meet you." Said Jack. "Well, we'd better be going to the airport Darlin'. Don't want to miss that flight. If I'm not back on time, my folks will kill me! I've got classes tomorrow at the JC. I'm going to Durham Technical. I'm gett'n an Associate's in Automotive Technical. I'm not as motivated as my little cookie here, but I'll be able to take care of her and our family real good. My family business is doin' real good now. But they wanted me to do better than just a high school degree."

TJ ran her hands through her hair, and straightened her little summer dress. She looked in the mirror and said, "Well, I'll be back in a jiffy. I'll just drop Jack Danger off and we'll study for that test when I get back, okay?"

"It was real nice meet'n you, Miss Julie. See ya."

Jack stepped out into the corridor and as she was leaving, TJ stuck her head in and said, "I'll tell you all the dirty details when I get back." She winked and Julie couldn't help but laugh.

Julie could totally see what the attraction to Jack Danger was all about. He was real nice-looking in a redneck sort of way. Very polite, and very attractive. He had huge shoulders and a tiny waist.

Julie threw her bag on the bed, and as she unpacked, she decided she would write a letter to Brian to explain how she felt about their first time having sex. She let him know what she needed from him as far as getting her to feel comfortable doing it again, and told him that she wanted to work on their relationship in a deeper way. She did miss him and couldn't wait to see him again. But she felt she didn't want these things to go unsaid before he came home. She wanted to get it off her chest so when they saw each other it wouldn't be awkward for her. After being around TJ and the other women in the dorm, she pretty much had an idea what she thought she wanted to get her to the point the others were at so the experience would be what she had envisioned. Everyone was always talking about what their lovers were doing and how much sex was a pleasurable thing. Julie wanted this more than anything. It just hadn't been a priority to her up until now. Now along with her studies, she needed a release as well. And she wanted it to be with Brian.

Chapter 5

$\mathcal{J}$ ulie and TJ sat in their caps and gowns waiting for their names to be called to walk onto the stage and receive their bachelor degrees. TJ was leaving the next morning to return to North Carolina. She had received a 178 score on her LSAT and had been accepted to Duke University to attend law school. She was planning her wedding to Jack Danger in December and would continue school during that time. It was going to be a huge event at her grandfather's estate. Being a judge, he would be officiating. The estate had been a tobacco plantation that was several hundred years old. They raised horses on the property now and it had amazing gardens. Julie and her parents were planning to attend, and Julie was to be the maid of honor. She had received a 180 on her LSAT, and had decided to go back to San Diego to attend the School of Law at Scripps Ranch. This would put her closer to home and closer to the Camp Pendleton base where Brian was still stationed. He had already gone overseas twice. They hadn't planned to marry until Julie finished school. Theirs was to be a small wedding.

In May 1988, Julie graduated from law school with a degree in Criminal Justice. And in October the next year at the age of twenty-four, she and Brian were married between deployments.

Julie wasn't much for a fuss, and just wanted family and close friends to be present. Brian's father, however, insisted on a Marine Corps presence at the ceremony. It was held on base at a small chapel, in the presence of only about thirty people. Julie insisted on a simple tea-length white dress and no veil. Brian looked very handsome in full uniform as he placed a thin gold band on Julie's finger.

Things between them were okay now, but he seemed to be changing a bit every time he left and came back. She had discussed this with her mom, but they both agreed it was probably just his growing up and maturing. And perhaps, she just hadn't noticed having had her nose in her books for the last five years. But still, something in the back of Julie's mind cautioned her. He seemed to be a bit withdrawn and things seemed a bit off.

Julie had stuck to her goal and managed to get through college and law school in five years. TJ and JD had flown in for the wedding. She had also graduated from Duke, and was as big as a house. They were expecting twin boys the following month. TJ was planning on taking a year off to stay home with the boys. They were still as happy and in love as always.

Julie and Brian didn't have much time as a married couple. He was to leave in January to go to the Middle East. He couldn't discuss much of what he was doing with Julie or his family. But they all understood. He was a member of some

Special Forces group within the Marine Corps. Maybe that was adding to his silence and moodiness. Brian assured Julie that it wasn't anything to do with her. He just had a lot on his mind.

Brian and Julie found a cute two-bedroom duplex on F Street on Coronado Island across the bay from San Diego. A big bridge connected the mainland to the island. Brian had been transferred to the Naval Amphibious Base there in Coronado where the Navy Seals trained, and Julie had been hired by a big law office there. She was going to work for a big-time lawyer by the name of Bernard Rosenthal. A real feather in her cap as jobs go. He was one of the 'good old boys' in the law circles. Mr. Rosenthal reminded her of a big Texan. He stood six feet six inches tall and was a bit big around the middle. His stature was intimidating. He always wore a vest with his suits, and had a pocket watch he would take out and look at when he was attempting to look bored. Having been in practice for more than thirty years, he had represented very wealthy clients. He loved being in the limelight and getting lots of attention. He was always in the press. She would be there until she passed the bar exam, and then she was going to just take it one day at a time.

Brian would come home in the evening and not talk much to Julie. He seemed to become more and more distant every day. He had never been great in the sack, but even that was getting less and less frequent. It didn't seem to interest him no matter what she tried. She was becoming very frustrated. She seemed to have finally come into her sexual peak, and he wasn't participating.

When January came, Brian was sent to the Middle East again. He was to return later that year. Julie and TJ talked on the phone at least twice a week. They had remained best friends and were each other's confidantes. She confessed to TJ that she was actually feeling relieved that he had been deployed again, and she didn't really feel guilty about it. She wanted to focus on studying for the bar. His absence gave her more time to do that without having to feel like she was walking on egg shells. The more time passed, the more distant Brian became. She would try to explain to him that he wasn't being very attentive, and he would apologize. He would be okay for a day or two, and then go back into his mood. Not having been with anyone else, she wished she had found the kind of relationship that her best friend had with her husband.

When Julie started working for Mr. Rosenthal, she spent most of her time doing research for the practice. She didn't mind. That gave her time alone in that big and busy office. Often times, she would drive in to San Diego during a big case and watch the lawyers going at it. Some of them were great, and some were mediocre. At times, she would watch the prosecutors in action and take notes on things they said. She was leaning in that direction when she passed the bar. She found it fascinating how easy Mr. Rosenthal made it look when he got some scumbag rich kid off with just warnings for drunk driving or possession. In the back of her mind, she made mental notes of the way he played the game. She figured that would help her in the future when she was on the prosecution side. She hated being blindsided during debates, and this was pretty much a game of pawns, too. Being able to anticipate what the defense team would use to try to acquit their clients would make her a better prosecutor.

Mr. Rosenthal had several partners. One which was his oldest son Reginald. He was a balding man in his early forties who specialized in high-profile divorce cases. The other two practiced financial fraud and defended different types of cases. Some involving estate disputes, of which there were plenty in the area. There were many retired Navy and Marine officers on the island and in the surrounding areas who were being taken to the cleaners by their wives after finding out their husbands had been less than faithful. Those were the bread and butter cases for the practice.

All of the partners had assistants, including Mr. Rosenthal. His assistant was also the office manager. Her name was Pearl Parker. She'd been with Rosenthal since he started his practice. 'Ms.' Parker was a late-fiftyish old maid who had a stick so far up her butt it would take an autopsy to remove it. Always with a bun on top of her salt and pepper hair, she wore suits that looked like they had been in her wardrobe since Sears and Roebuck opened for business. She was very frugal. She always brought her lunch in a paper bag that she reused, and drove a white Chevy Impala from the 1960s.

Julie hated it when she would creep up behind her while she was working in her cubicle. She did it to sneak a peek at what she was working on and to make sure she was concentrating on only office work and nothing personal.

After work, Julie would go home and put on her bathrobe and slippers. She'd call her mom and dad to check on them. Then, she would go through the mail. Rarely there would be a letter from Brian. He used to write to her all the time when they were younger. But now she was lucky to get a postcard. He said he was too busy with his military operations and didn't ever get near the mail room to buy stamps. Supposedly, he was always outside somewhere. Probably hiding under some bush or up a tree. Who knew? Sometimes she would send him a card just to maintain some kind of communication. The last time he came home, she found two of her cards in his duffle bag still unopened. She was starting to wonder if he even cared about her anymore. It seemed like the Corps was his wife, and that his friends were his family.

Brian came home that year in November. Julie was excited to have him see how the apartment had turned out. He'd left so shortly after they moved in, she hadn't really done any decorating.

They managed to purchase a bed at the Navy Exchange when they moved in. She was to pick everything else out later by herself. He had no interest in home décor. They were planning on going to his parents' home in La Jolla for Thanksgiving. Her mom and dad would also be there, as would Brian's older brother Chuck, who would be flying in from Virginia.

Brian seemed disinterested in the décor, and in anything else she had done. He seemed to make only polite conversation. She had wanted to make love the first night he was home, but he made the excuse that the flight had worn him out. He would take a rain check. This made her angry and sad at the same time. He rolled over and began to snore. She crept out into the living room and stepped outside into the front porch to sit on the picnic bench and look at the night sky. She began to cry while asking the stars why her husband didn't love her anymore. What was she to do? She sobbed for a long time. She knew she deserved better than this and wished she had never let Brian talk her into believing that he was going to love her and take care of her forever. She wished she had experienced more relationships while she was away at school so she would have something to compare to. And she wished she hadn't said, *'Till death do us part.'* She knew she deserved something bet-ter…something more. Her heart felt empty.

In the morning, he was up at the crack of dawn and off to the base without even telling her he was leaving. He thought she was asleep and didn't know she'd been awake all night. Julie looked at the clock and knew it was okay to call TJ. The East Coast was three hours ahead and she knew if it was six A.M. there, it was nine in Raleigh. And those twin boys had probably gotten her up at the crack of dawn.

TJ answered the phone and heard nothing but sobbing on the other end. She knew it was her sweet friend who needed a hug. Or at the very least, an ear. When Julie finished tell-ing her what had transpired the night before, TJ told her she only had two options. "Hang in there, or walk away." She told Julie she was "too young not to leave him before he completely destroyed her spirit." She would find someone more worthy of her and all of her love."

After an hour, Julie hung up and got ready for work. The office was closing early today because many of the employees were leaving town early to drive to be with family for the Thanksgiving holiday the next day. When Julie got home at four, Brian was already there.

"What time do you want to leave in the morning to go to my folks?" he asked as if nothing was wrong. He seemed normal for that moment.

"Whenever you think. But it should be early so your folks can spend as much time with you as possible. I know they've missed you."

"Okay. I'm going to go back to the base for a while to hang out with the guys. We're going to go to the bar on base and throw back a few beers. You don't mind, do you?"

He didn't even give her a chance to reply. He picked up the keys to his truck, kissed her on the forehead, and was gone out the door before she could even protest.

Julie went into the kitchen to put together a cobbler she was going to take in the morning for the dinner. As she stood working in the kitchen, tears welled up behind her piercing blue eyes and slowly began to rolling down her face. She felt invisible and alone. Very alone.

In the morning when she got up, Brian was snoring on the couch, reeking of beer and alcohol. Julie went into the kitchen to make coffee. Brian must have heard her and he came in to see what she was doing.

"What's all the racket?" he asked while scratching himself. "Sorry I got in so late. I didn't want to wake you up so I just crashed on the couch." Brian walked to where Julie stood at the sink and pushed up against her. She was surprised to feel his erection behind her. He kissed Julie on the side of the neck and ran his hands around to the front of her night gown. He began to squeeze her breasts and lick the side of her neck. Julie didn't know what to think. He so rarely showed her any affection.

"Are you horny?" he whispered in her ear. "You wanna get laid?" Julie turned to face him and all she could smell was the booze from the night before. He continued to kiss the side of her neck and she turned her face to try to avoid the disgusting aroma. Brian picked Julie up and sat her on the kitchen table. He unbuttoned his pants and pushed her nightgown up around her waist. Julie hadn't been touched in such a long time, she knew she'd be slow to react. Getting turned on came with effort for her, and he was never very good at helping. She reached down and used her fingers to try to manipulate and lubricate herself. That was never a priority of Brian's. She tried to move quickly because she knew what was coming. He exposed himself and began pushing against her until he got all the way in. He was always in such a hurry to relieve himself, he never considered her needs. Brian pushed Julie down onto the table and grabbed her toward him by the underside of her thighs. He went at her like a piece of meat. Julie laid there and the memory of their first time together flashed back into her mind. *This isn't making love.* She thought to herself. *This is just screwing.*

Brian came quickly and like always, pulled out and zipped himself up. He helped Julie sit up and as he turned and walked away said, "I'm taking a shower so we can go. Be sure you're ready. We can only stay for a bit. I don't want to get caught up I traffic. I need to be on base tomorrow at 0500."

Julie just sat there. It all happened so quickly she didn't know what hit her. There was no love there. She may as well get him a blow-up doll to use. That's what she felt like. Not a wife who was loved and cherished, but an object to be used whenever he decided he needed it.

Chapter 6

When Brian and Julie arrived at her in-laws' home, her parents were already there. Chuck heard Brian's truck pull into the driveway and ran out to greet them. He ran over to open Julie's door and help her out. Then, he ran over to Brian's side of the truck and put his arms around him and lifted him off the ground, twirling him.

"Hey little brother, good to see you man!" He put his arm around Brian and they walked ahead into the house. Julie pulled the cobbler out of the truck and followed them in. Julie understood the affection Brian was being shown and all, but she couldn't help feel a bit out of place.

Julie's mom came up to hug her and took the cobbler into the kitchen to put on the buffet. Then they all went into the living room and sat listening to Brian, Chuck, and the Colonel talk Marine Corps. She couldn't wait to get the hell out of there. She was sick of hearing nothing but Marine Corps talk every time Brian was home. No one asked about her career. No one asked if they were happy and how the apartment was coming along, or about their marriage.

Brian, Chuck, and the Colonel discussed the recent bombings overseas, and how Brian and Chuck couldn't wait to get a piece of the real action. Brian's mom was hitting the wine bottle like usual. Julie figured it was her way of coping. It seemed she always had to maintain her buzz whenever they all got together. She was always walking around with a wine glass in one hand and a cigarette in the other. Who could blame her? This was all she'd heard all of her life. She must have felt like wallpaper.

After supper, Brian said they had to leave. He excused them from the table and told Julie to get in the truck. He said nothing to her on the way home, and when they got home, he undressed himself and crawled into bed. He managed to say "good night" and rolled over, only to begin snoring the minute his head was turned onto the pillow.

After a week of Brian leaving for the base before the roosters crowed, and coming home later and later, he announced he'd be leaving in three days to go somewhere in the Middle East. He couldn't say where, just that his small team was being deployed overseas, and he had no clue as to when he would be coming back. He seemed excited and pumped when he called his father to give him the news. He didn't even ask Julie how she felt about the whole thing. Military wives expect their husbands to be called away periodically. But it seemed that Brian was called away more often than not. She was sad about being alone again and not having time with her husband to be newlyweds, or to work on their marriage. Julie drove him to the Amphibious Base on Coronado early in the morning that

Friday. He couldn't wait to get out of the car. He leaned over and kissed Julie on the cheek and didn't even look back. She watched as he walked toward the quarterdeck with his duffle bag on his back. She didn't even shed a tear. She realized that he had managed to drain the love out of her, or the desire to even care anymore. She even welcomed the loneliness.

Everyone knew in August that Operation Desert Storm was going on, and at that time, no one knew just how long it was all going to last. Most people thought it was going to be a short war with minimal casualties. President Bush had been waiting until mid-January to see if the Iraqis would pull out of Kuwait by their deadline. But the deadline passed and the airstrikes began. Iraq had attacked Israel with missiles, and the Desert Storm war phase began in full force. Julie didn't know exactly where Brian was, but she suspected he was somewhere in Kuwait. By the end of February, it had officially come to an end, but there was more to be done. She knew he wouldn't be home for some time. She had received correspondence from the office of the Secretary of Defense letting her know that her husband was safe, and that they would keep her notified of any further information as it became declassified and available for release.

Julie buried herself in her studies and her work. She enjoyed working in the law practice of Mr. Rosenthal. He had begun to show interest in her completed assignments, and told her she showed "great promise." This infuriated Ms. Parker who wasn't happy when he would call Julie into his office to discuss law practice or cases with her behind closed doors. She detested not being included in things. All that made her especially rude to Julie. But that didn't faze Julie. She just kept her nose in her work. She had no time for the old bitty.

In April, Julie took the bar exam and passed with flying colors. She was so excited, she brought the results in to share with Mr. Rosenthal, who immediately sent Ms. Parker out to get a cake and some champagne. The office conference room was full of celebration and champagne glasses were clinking. Ms. Parker stayed at her desk and didn't want to participate. She picked up her purse and left early that day.

Julie hurried home to call her parents and TJ, who was getting ready to take her test the following month. Taking care of twins was becoming a full-time job, and not one she had envisioned for herself. She loved the boys but she was ready to get to work. Her daddy and big brother had used her periodically for research for their law firm as well, but couldn't wait to have her in the practice. The boys were old enough now to leave at home with the Au Pair they had hired. She'd been with them now for about four months so TJ could study. The boys loved her, and she seemed to really love them.

Julie spent that weekend at her parents' house. Her mom and dad wanted some quality time with her, and her dad had invited family over for a barbecue to celebrate. Julie welcomed the distraction since she'd done nothing but study for what seemed like forever.

Everyone in the family was talking about the young high school teacher who had been arrested that week for allegedly having three of her seventeen-year-old male students kill her husband in exchange for sex. She had supposedly promised to marry one of them if he would shoot and kill her husband. They all wanted Julie's opinion as to whether she thought the woman was guilty and if she thought she would go to prison. But she'd been so busy studying for that exam, that she hadn't heard all of the details.

That next Monday morning, Julie tried to find a parking spot near her office on Orange Avenue, the main street on Coronado Island. There wasn't an empty spot for blocks. She didn't know what was going on. As she drove past the office, there were television news reporters and their vans parked everywhere, including up on the sidewalks. They were running around with microphones all over the place. She had to walk four blocks back to the office building, which had at one time been someone's big residence.

"What the hell is going on?" She thought as she fought her way through the crowd of people, blocking her path as she tried to get to the front door which she found locked.

"What do you have to say about the case, Miss? Are you employed by Mr. Rosenthal or are you a client?" So many questions were being thrown at her as she tried to get in. She pounded on the door, and finally Ms. Parker came and unlocked it and she quickly scooted in.

"Ms. Parker, what on earth is going on?" She said as she walked in the direction of her cubicle.

"Mr. Rosenthal is waiting for you in the conference room. The others have already arrived. You're late," she snarled at Julie and she turned and walked away.

Julie dropped her purse and briefcase, grabbed a note pad and headed straight into the conference room. All of the attorneys and their assistants were already seated. As she walked in and took a seat, she said, "I'm so sorry, I wasn't able to find any place to park. I had to go a long way and then walked up. The crowd wouldn't let me get to the door without mobbing me. What happen? Did someone die?"

Mr. Rosenthal stood and pulled down on his vest. "Well little lady, I guess you don't listen to the news much. Have you heard about the Pamela Dean case?"

"Oh, is that the school teacher who slept with a couple of her students and one of them shot and killed her husband?"

"*Allegedly* slept with her students. Well, I've decided to take the case myself. I met with her at the jail this weekend."

"But she has no money," protested Reginald. "She is an underpaid school teacher whose husband was unemployed. How are we supposed to get paid for that?"

"Now, you let me worry about that, son," said Mr. Rosenthal as he took a seat. "You see, this is one case we need for the publicity. I have enough money and so do all of you. But what we don't have so much of is free press and exposure. Yes, we are well known in these parts. But outside of this area, we are just another hot-shot law firm. I want this practice to be the foremost law firm in all of California. I'd like to get some of that Hollywood business in here." He looked at the other partners and pointed his finger at them and said, "Wouldn't you like to represent some of those 'hotsy-totsy' celebrities and get your names in the paper all over the U.S.?"

Everyone in the room just looked around at everyone else. "I'm taking this case pro bono. And there's a reason for my so-called madness. I'm going to write a book about it! At least, I'm going to have someone help me do the writing and I'm going to tell them what to say. One of those ghost writers. Think of the money I'll make from selling the book. And I'll leave a legacy for my family and the practice will get tons of exposure. You'll all make even more money! Now, I know this place will be a zoo for a while. But just bear with me. Go on about your business. Sit back, relax, and listen to the phone ring. I'll do all the talking, is that clear? No one else in this office has any comment. No one!"

The room was silent. No one offered anything to say. They were all sitting around the table with their mouths wide open. Mr. Rosenthal stood and looked right at Julie. He pointed his finger at her and said, "You, in my office now." With that, he stood and walked out.

Julie followed Mr. Rosenthal into his office and he asked her to close the door. She did so and sat across his desk and he paced up and down in front of his window, looking at all the reporters.

"Now Miss Julie," he said as he finally sat on his huge leather chair. "I'm going to ask that you help me with this case. I know you have license in hand, but I don't believe you have had any offers to go anywhere anytime soon, am I right?"

"No, sir. That hasn't even crossed my mind just yet. I'm still trying to wrap my head around having passed the bar. I'm in no hurry to go anywhere."

"Good, good," he said as he leaned over and pushed the button by his telephone summoning Ms. Parker into his office. She quickly stepped in with an envelope in her hand and handed it to him.

"Is this what you called me in here for?" she asked as she turned to give Julie a dirty look.

"Yes, thank you. That'll be all." He waved his hand at her in a dismissive manner.

"Now Julie, here is an offer from me and this firm. Now, take a look at it and let me know if you think this starting salary is going to be sufficient for your services. Now keep in mind, you are still wearing Pampers and you're wet behind the ears. It might not be as much as you might be expecting. But you still have some experience to gain, and I'm here to help you with that as much as you need. I see great promise in you. Your work for us so far has been excellent. I know you'll be excellent in your practice of law in the future. That's why I would like you to consider staying with us here. There's also going to be an additional bonus after this trial is over because you'll have to spend some extra time still doing even more research. But you have proven to be very thorough so far. I'll need that in this case. Now, go ahead and open it."

Julie could hardly believe her ears. He was offering her a job! Julie took a deep breath and tore open the envelope. She was being offered fifty thousand dollars annually right out of law school, plus bonuses. That was more than she had expected to get any place. It was a lot of money for anyone in those days.

"Mr. Rosenthal!" she said.

"Oh now, you have to start calling me Bernie. Everyone else here calls me Bernie. We can't be formal if we're going to work together. But not Ms. Parker, you understand. Only the associates can call me Bernie."

Julie smiled and stood up to shake his hand. "Bernie, I accept! Thank you so very much. I'll work hard. You know I will."

Mr. Rosenthal laughed. "Well, welcome aboard. Now let me tell you what's going to happen. First of all, I've hired a ghost writer. He'll be here some time tomorrow. He's a friend of my brother's up in the Hollywood. Did you know my brother was a producer? Well, I met this young man at a Hanukkah party at my Brother Julian's house. Nice young man. Went to USC School of Journalism. Top of his class. Anyway, he was working at one of the local news stations and they tightened up their belts and let him and a bunch of other people go. So he was writing for TV shows, doing some ghost writing and such until he decides his next move. When I met him, he told me if I ever needed a writer to call. So I did. Ms. Parker has found him a guest house behind a residence on Isabella Street where he'll be staying for the duration. I'll expect you to show him around and cooperate with him as much as he needs. I want him to get every bit of information as things progress. The book will be released after the case closes. He knows that his confidence is very important. I trust him. His name is Alex Hart. Are we clear on this?"

Julie had been sitting there still trying to take it all in. She nodded and said, "Yes, of course. Whatever you need, sir. And thank you for the opportunity. I'm very grateful for the job."

"Now, go dig up as much as you can on this Dean woman and her dead husband. And see what you can get on the kid that shot him and the other delinquents."

Julie stood up to walk to the door. As she put her hand on the doorknob, she got a glimpse of Ms. Parker who had been sitting outside the door at her desk trying to eavesdrop through the closed glass door. As Julie walked past her to her desk, she saw that she quickly turned her head the other way. *What the hell is her problem anyway? Busy body!* Julie thought to herself.

As the day progressed, Bernie asked Julie and several of the other lawyers to step outside with him. He was going to hold a press conference. When they walked out the door onto the front steps, the flashes were blinding. The press was so loud, Bernie could hardly get a word in edge-wise. When it was finally over, most of them packed up and left for the day. They had gotten what they came for.

That evening, the news was all a-chatter about the case. A young, attractive schoolteacher in her late twenties allegedly used her students for sex and to carry out a murder. Julie could see why Bernie jumped at the case for publicity. It was going to be a wild ride.

Chapter 7

When Julie arrived at her home late that evening, she was still trying to digest the day. She was in the kitchen putting away a few groceries she had stopped to buy and looked around at mess. She'd been so busy she hadn't had much time to clean up while Brian was home. He was always very messy and never did anything to help. She decided to go change, call her mom and TJ, and then do some house cleaning.

As she closed the last cabinet, she heard the phone ring in the living room. It was her mom. She'd seen the news and had seen Julie on TV during the news conference. Julie gave her the big news about the job offer with the practice. Her mom was excited and was congratulating her when Julie heard her 'call waiting' alert and knew there was another call coming in. She told her mom she'd call her later in the week and switched lines. It was TJ.

"Hey girlfriend! You look mighty cute on TV!" she shouted with a giggle. They both laughed and Julie gave her friend the news about the job offer. "I couldn't be happier for you, darlin'," she told her friend with her usual Southern drawl. "You hit the jack pot with this case, girl! This is a great way to start your career. I hope I can pass that bar next month. I'm so nervous! I just keep say'n 'Jesus take the wheel!'"

"I'm excited and nervous at the same time. I just hope I can live up to Bernie's expectations," said Julie.

"Oh, so it's Bernie now…you go, girl. Well, call me soon and fill me in on the details. Now you know they're going to find that hussy guilty as sin. But I'm sure your boss will put on quite a show. Good luck with everything. Love you. Bye-bye."

Julie was so happy and excited. She couldn't possibly go to bed. She decided she'd turn on all the lights and clean the whole house. She had really neglected it with her studies and was determined some housework was just what the doctor ordered. She dusted and vacuumed and cleaned the kitchen. When she got to the bathroom, she was scrubbing the tub when she heard a clinking noise. She looked down to her hands and realized her wedding band was gone!

"Oh shit! Oh no! What am I going to do?" She looked at the clock. It was after midnight.

No one would come out at this late hour. She decided to call someone first thing in the morning.

Right at eight, she called and left a message at work saying she had an emergency and would be in as soon as possible. Then she began to call and finally found a plumber who was there within thirty minutes. The man stuck a hose with a camera on the end down the drain. He looked and looked, but told Julie it was gone. There was nothing he could do.

"Had it gone down the sink, I may have been able to retrieve it. But the tub has a straight down drain and it's probably halfway to the main sewer and on its way to the ocean by now. I'm sorry, lady."

As Julie drove to the office, she didn't know what to think or what she felt. Maybe it was a sign. After all, TJ had told her that her marriage to Brian sounded like it was in the toilet anyway. She figured she had plenty of time to decide what to do. She could always go buy and new one at the Exchange on base where they purchased the ring anyway. It's not like it had cost a lot of money.

When Julie arrived at the office, there were only a couple of news vans there. No one was even outside. As she sat at her desk, she looked across the room and saw someone sitting in front of the desk from her boss. Trying to put the morning's event behind her, she began trying to gather her thoughts by making an outline of what she was going to do, and the information she thought she was going to need first when her intercom line rang. It was Bernie asking her to step into his office.

Julie let herself in and was invited to sit down on the chair next to where the other guest was. "Julie, I want you to meet Alex Hart. He's going to help co-write my book." Julie turned to shake hands with the guest. When she looked up at his face, she couldn't help but notice the striking, emerald-colored eyes and the sandy blonde hair. He was much younger than she had expected.

"How do you do?" he said with a big grin. "I'm told you are terrific at your job and you're going to be my right-hand person while I'm here. It'll be nice getting to know you," he said as he squeezed her hand a bit too tightly for her comfort.

"It will be my pleasure," she said as she withdrew her hand and felt her cheeks become flush for no apparent reason. It was embarrassing for her. She had never reacted like that to anyone before.

"I need you to show Mr. Hart to his new digs," said Bernie. "It's not too far, down on Isabella Street. Ms. Parker picked up the keys yesterday. She gave them to Mr. Hart with the address. Since he's never been to Coronado before, you might just drive him around and point out restaurants, banks, dry cleaners, you know…important stuff."

Julie hadn't expected to spend her day being a tour guide. She had a lot of work to do and protested to her boss. "Mr. Rosenthal, I mean, Bernie, I have a lot of work to do today. I really need to get started on our investigation. Perhaps Ms. Parker can show Mr. Hart around, or one of the other clerks. I was going to start downtown today at the County Clerk's office looking at records."

"Oh, there's plenty of time for that. The trial isn't even going to start for months. Better you give this young man a quick tour today. You wouldn't really want to subject him to Ms. Parker would you? Start by showing him his apartment. I hear it's a very nicely furnished guest house. The owners aren't around. They are in Europe somewhere. He'll probably want to do some unpacking and he might to go to the store or something. Now, go on. And oh, by the way, the arraignment is at two tomorrow afternoon. You should both be there."

Julie's cheeks were still feeling flush and knew Alex was aware of her reaction to him. She just wanted to get to her desk and hide from him. But instead, she was being forced to drag him around. She wasn't happy at all, but he seemed very pleased that she would be the one showing him around.

As they left Bernie's office, Alex opened the door for Julie. She headed straight for her desk. Alex headed over to Ms. Parker's desk. He smiled at her and picked up her hand.

"Ms. Parker, I hope you have a lovely day. Thank you for all of your help. You've been just wonderful. I look forward to working with you." He kissed Ms. Parker's hand and Julie saw that she blushed and smiled like she'd never seen. He was obviously a ladies' man and knew who he was going to have to butter up to.

Alex walked over to Julie's desk and as he approached, she picked up her car keys, turned, and began to walk in the direction of the front door. As he held it open for her, he asked "So, where to first?"

"Well, we might consider the Emergency room first. A Rabies shot might be good just about now."

Once in her car, she asked for the address to his guest house.

"It's 1151 Isabella. Do you know where that is?"

"I know where Isabella is. It's right off of this main street. Orange Avenue is the Main Street in town. Don't think of speeding here, either. The cops around here don't have much to do, so they watch for anyone going over the speed limit by even one mile."

"Well, I know a good attorney. Maybe she can fix my ticket," he said as he smiled at her.

Alex was very drawn to Julie. Her shiny long brown hair and her skin was silky smooth. Those big beautiful long eyelashes made her deep blue eyes seem huge.

"Here is Isabella Street," she said as she made a right turn. "Now, what's the address again?"

"1151. I think it's going to be here on the right. There it is, on the corner. That big pink house."

"You're lucky," she said. "You're only a block up from the beach."

Julie turned into the big circular driveway. They both got out of the car and Alex told Julie that Ms. Parker had told him to go to the gate on the right of the house and just walk on into the back. As he held the gate open, Julie stepped in ahead of him. "Wow! What a nice yard. Can you believe this place?" he said. "There, that must be the cottage. I don't see another one back here, do you?"

Julie rolled her eyes back and followed him down the brick path in the direction of the small pink cottage. It was a lovely yard. Rose bushes and Azaleas lined the walkways. The Calla lilies were just starting to pop. Alex turned the key and swung the door open. It was furnished with a woman's touch in mind. The couches were flower prints and the walls had a light pink tone with a wallpaper trim adorned with roses across the top. The living room-kitchen combination was spacious, and there was a nice fireplace. The bedroom was off the living room and was also very feminine.

"Well, this will do, I guess. It's just temporary. Not my taste, but it will do," he said.

Julie watched him as he inspected the rooms. He was very attractive. He had on a light caramel-colored suit, a white shirt, and a green tie that set off his eyes. His sandy blonde hair sat just over his ears, and he had a great smile. She caught herself checking him out and shook her head.

"Well, I'll show you a couple of things and then take you back to the office. You can pick up your car and make your way back so you can unpack. The grocery store is on the way, you'll see it. Can't really get lost in this town. There is not much to it and most everything you need is on the main street. If you go too far on Orange Avenue, you'll drive right into the water."

"You're terrific. Thanks."

On the way back to the office, Julie drove him by the bakery, the coffee shop, and pointed out a couple of stores. Alex sat in the car and stared at Julie all the way back to the office. She caught him looking at her out of the corner of her eye. She noticed herself blushing again and was anxious to just get there.

"How about I buy you lunch to thank you for the tour?" he said when they were almost back to the office.

"No, thanks. I have a lot to do. I think you should just go back and get settled, don't you? And you might want to stay clear of Old Lady Parker. She doesn't like anybody that takes Mr. Rosenthal's attention off of her. She's a nosy old bitty."

Alex gave her a big grin that almost melted her right there in her seat. "You just leave old Pearl to me. I'll have her eating out of my hand in no time."

Julie went in and sat at her desk to continue to work on her outline. She saw Alex step into Bernie's office for a minute and then walk back to the front. She looked down as he approached her cubicle. She didn't want him to catch her staring at him.

"Are you sure I can't buy you lunch today? I mean, we're going to be working very closely and we should get to know one another."

"No thanks. I have a ton of work to prepare for my investigation and I have to go downtown to dig through some records," she said without looking up at him. She just couldn't look up at him without getting nervous.

"Well, all right then. Some other time perhaps," he said as he tapped on her desk and walked out the door.

When he left, Julie realized she hadn't been breathing. She had to sit back, take a deep breath and a drink of water. Her palms were moist. What was it about this guy? He really was sort of irritating, and much too Hollywood for her to even give him a second thought. But he obviously had some sort of effect on her. She didn't really like it. It interrupted her focus.

When she got home that evening, she called TJ to tell her that she'd lost her wedding ring down the drain and about his annoying man she was going to have to put up with for the duration of the trial, and how he would demand a lot of her attention because he'd be following her around during the process so he could get his information. TJ's response was, "It's a sign girlfriend, I'm telling you, it's a sign! Watch out, Darlin'. That Mr. Hollywood might just be the one that steals your heart away. Sometimes they're right under our noses and we just don't know it. Watch and see."

"Oh nonsense, he is going to be a pain in my butt, I just know it."

"Don't you worry. I'll be telling you 'I told you so' before you know it," laughed TJ.

Chapter 8

When the alarm rang at six thirty, Julie jumped onto her feet and hit the shower. She hadn't decided what to wear, so she took extra time looking through her closet. Recently, she had purchased some new suits and found herself changing her mind several times. Her makeup was applied extra perfectly this morning, and she tied her hair back with a new clip. She told herself it had nothing to do with Mr. Hollywood, and that she just wanted to look good in court today. But in the back of her mind, she wondered about what TJ had said to her the previous night. After trying on two of the new outfits, she settled on a light blue pin stripe suit and a white blouse.

When she got to the office at seven forty-five, she went straight to her desk. Julie always liked getting there ahead of the crowd and getting settled for her day. As she emptied her briefcase, she saw something out of the corner of her eye pop up from behind the cubicle divider to her left.

"Good morning, Sunshine!" It was Alex. He walked around to her side and placed a small glass on her desk with some of the Azaleas from his garden.

"What is that?" she asked, half smiling.

"Just a little thank you for taking the time to show me around yesterday. And I have something else, too." He walked back to his new cubicle next to hers and handed her a small white paper bag. "I went to the bakery this morning and picked up some doughnut holes. Do you know that a dozen doughnut holes is only fifty cents here? In L.A., they would cost you ninety nine cents a dozen. I guess the ritzy people in your town don't like them and they are practically giving them away! I thought we could start the morning off with coffee and a little breakfast. How do you like your coffee?"

"Oh, that's not necessary, really," said Julie, trying not to smile. "I don't usually eat breakfast."

Alex walked back over to her desk and placed his hands on his waist. "Don't you know that breakfast is the most important meal of the day? And today is a very special day. You have to be on your best game. Come on, it's just coffee and doughnut holes."

Julie finally gave in to his pleading and smiled. She found him irresistible and irritating at the same time. "All right. If it'll get you to leave me alone. I do really have a lot of preparation to do for this afternoon and I plan to work through the morning."

She stood up and walked to the break room. Alex followed right behind her. "I made the coffee just a little while ago. How do you take it?"

"I can get my own coffee," she protested and walked over to the coffee pot. Alex poured his and sat across from where she had sat, and emptied the doughnut holes onto a napkin. The break room was the original kitchen of the home the office was now occupying. It had belonged to a wealthy doctor who had it built when he retired from the Navy. He designed it so that the bottom of the home was his office and the upstairs was the apartment he shared with his wife. Now, the upstairs was used as conference rooms, storage, and filing rooms.

"So, are you a dunker or a dipper?" He asked as he picked up the first doughnut hole and dunked it into his coffee.

Julie laughed and dunked hers as well, placing the whole thing in her mouth. "I'm a dunker, but I have to be careful today. I can't get my blouse dirty."

"Ah, a woman after my own heart. Not too many ladies would admit to being dunkers. They're always trying to appear so lady-like all the while, being closet dunkers. I like a woman who will admit to it right off. It shows you have self-confidence and don't mind people knowing where you stand right off the bat. I'm impressed."

"Don't be. I just am who I am. I've never had time for games of any kind. Except for the ones we play in the court room. Which reminds me, I have to get to work."

Right after Julie finished her sentence, Pearl Parker walked into the kitchen and stopped dead in her tracks. She looked at the two of them with disapproval and walked over to the coffee pot.

"Good morning Ms. Parker. Don't you look lovely today?" said Alex with that big smile of his. Julie picked up her coffee mug and exited the room. Alex offered Ms. Parker a doughnut hole but she declined, walking straight back to her desk and sitting in her chair with her perfect posture. Alex picked up his mug and began to walk back into the large room full of cubicles and people. He stood in the doorway and stared at Julie while he finished his coffee. He saw something different in her. Something that stirred his insides. He'd been in a relationship with someone that hadn't ended well. Alex had discovered that his live-in girlfriend of two years had been carrying on with one of the news directors at the TV station where he worked, just before Thanksgiving. He swore to himself he would remain alone for at least one year before getting involved again. He'd wanted to spend some time alone to recharge his heart and do some soul searching. But this woman was engaging to him. He liked how she made him feel when he touched her hand. It was like a jolt or a current that had made him pay attention to her. The way she moved, the way she smiled. Something he couldn't put his finger on yet, but he knew she did something to him. So at that moment, he decided to go for it. He'd take it slow and just enjoy the ride.

"I have to meet with Bernie this morning to share some notes for the book," he told Julie. "Can we ride together to the courtroom this afternoon?"

Julie sighed. "I suppose so. But if you aren't here when I'm ready to go, you'll have to go on your own." Julie looked up at Alex and saw that he was staring at her with that irresistible smile as he sipped his coffee.

"Well, I'll just stick around until you're ready to go since I have no idea where the hell we're going. I'm counting on you to show me the ropes, okay?" Alex winked at Julie and walked around to his desk. He immediately began to hit the computer keys very quickly. He could obviously type very fast. Julie went back to her work and tried to do the same. She needed to concentrate. She had a report she had to give to Bernie as soon as he got in so he could use the information before the arraignment today. She also wanted to discuss hiring an investigator to help obtain information for the case.

Around nine-thirty, Julie looked up and saw that Bernie was in his office. She walked over to his door and saw that he was on the phone. She decided to stand outside until he was finished.

"He's on the phone," said Ms. Parker with a snarl.

"I can see that, thank you. I'll just wait right here until he's finished." Ms. Parker went back to whatever it was she was writing, making sure she didn't make eye contact with Julie. When Bernie was finished, he waved her in.

"Come on in Julie, come, and sit down. What do you have for me?" he said as he smiled.

"Well, I went downtown yesterday and got some general information from public records for you. Marriage certificates, property tax information, and such. Just the basic stuff."

Julie placed a file on Bernie's desk and he thumbed through it. "Excellent work as always. I knew I picked the right person for the job."

"I know you've suggested we use an investigator in the past for digging around people's work, so I thought we might use the same one we used for the Knudsen's case to see what he can dig up at the husband's work site. I'm going to go speak with the principal and talk to some of the teachers at the school where she worked, but I think perhaps the investigator would be a better fit for digging into the husband's circle of friends. Especially at his former work."

"I think you are on to something. Let's get him on the phone and sick him on them. He seems to have a way with that sort of thing. And I like how he works with all that undercover stuff. I'll leave that to you. How are you getting along with Mr. Hart?"

"Oh fine, fine. He's all right. He's going to ride into town with me to the court room this afternoon."

"Oh good, I'll have to go in to the city early. I'm having lunch with an old colleague before we go to the courthouse. He doesn't need to come along to listen to two old goats re-hashing our golf game."

Julie stood. As she turned to leave, Alex walked in, also with a file in his hands.

"Come in, Alex. Show me what you have so far." Bernie waved Alex in and he stood at the doorway to hold the door open for Julie. As she walked out, she saw him smiling at her. She passed so close to him that she couldn't help but take a whiff of the cologne he had on. Whatever it was, made her take a deep breath. It wasn't heavy. It was a light scent that made her stop for just a second to breathe it in. Most men's colognes smelled alike to her. They all smelled like musk. This one had a scent that made her weak in the knees.

As the door closed behind her, she stood there for a second trying to compose herself before trying to walk back to her desk. *What the hell is wrong with me? This has to stop! I'll never be able to get my work done like this.* She thought to herself and walked into the ladies room to throw cold water on her face.

As she stood there trying to compose herself she saw that she was red down to her neck. One of the attorneys' clerks walked in.

"Boy, are you lucky," she said to Julie. "I wish I was the one working with that Alex guy. How can you hold it together?"

"What do you mean?" asked Julie, full well knowing what she meant.

"He is a hunk. And he smells like heaven. Have you gotten a whiff of his cologne? It makes me want to jump his bones right here!" Julie looked in the mirror and tried to look unimpressed. She began to run her fingers through her hair and pretend to brush off her comments. "I just come here to do my work, not pick up on men. Besides, he's not my type." She turned and walked out of the ladies room and made her way back to her desk. Obviously she wasn't the only one who had noticed how attractive Alex was. She'd heard some of the other female employees chatting in the break room when she had stepped in to get coffee. They all seemed to be impressed by his good looks and sweet personality. This was just a distraction to her. The whole thing was a distraction. She didn't know what to think of it all and wondered if she could work through the whole thing, or if she, too, would be caught up in his charms.

Julie knew full well how unhappy she was in her marriage. She'd known for quite some time now that her marriage was not in her heart. It was something she had done because she felt like it was expected of her, and she didn't know better. But she questioned it now, especially after Brian's last time home. There was just nothing. No feeling in her heart. No love or even affection for him. She knew TJ was right. She deserved better. She wanted better, she needed more from a man. But she was afraid. She didn't want to disappoint her family and Brian's family by divorcing. She was lost in her feelings and her heart felt empty. That's why she had chosen to just bury herself in her work and tried not to think about it. But she knew it was something she would have to confront eventually. She just hadn't wanted to think about it. But *now* she was being forced to look deep inside. This man was forcing her to *feel* things she had never felt before. Now she knew what it was like to be really attracted to a man.

Chapter 9

The afternoon went off without a hitch. The arraignment came and went as Bernie had planned. There was a moment or two of grandstanding at the end where Bernie had all the reporters sticking cameras in his face, and he answered questions for them. Julie and Alex were in the background. Alex had gone to the courthouse with Julie just as he said, and it had messed with her nerves the entire time. Julie had tried to just keep the conversation to the case and to general stuff about Coronado Island. Alex kept trying to sway the conversation into a more personal one. But between answering calls from the office and taking the call from the investigator, she had succeeded in not having to give in to his questioning. She had set up a meeting with the investigator for the following day in the office so they could get a game plan.

It was late when they were finally finished, and on the way back across the bridge, Julie managed to just talk about the case with Alex. When they pulled up in front of the office, Julie didn't get out of the car.

"Aren't you coming in, Sunshine?" he asked.

"No, I'm tired and I have a big day tomorrow. I think I'll just get home and into the tub to try and relax a bit. I have to jot some thoughts down too, for the meeting with the investigator."

"Why don't you let me buy you dinner? You have to eat, don't you?"

"I'm really not hungry. I'll probably just make an omelet if I get hungry. But I just don't want to eat right now." Julie wasn't sure about accepting an invitation from Alex for dinner. She was embarrassed that he continued to pursue her. But it was getting harder to resist.

"I have to go back to L.A. in the morning. I won't be back until later in the week. You be sure and keep Ms. Parker's poison darts from landing anywhere near that pretty face of yours. See ya."

Alex stepped out of the car and closed the door behind him. Julie watched him walk over to his convertible and not even turn to look back once. As she drove away, she was puzzled. *What was he going back to Los Angeles for? Wasn't he supposed to stay here until the book was done? Did he have a girlfriend he was going to go see?* All these questions ran through her mind. *Was she picking up the wrong signal from him? Was he really not interested? Or was he just a player?*

When Julie got home, she poured herself a glass of wine, ran her tub full of hot water and crawled in. She had taken her portable phone in to call TJ to just check in.

"Hey girlfriend! Saw you on TV again today. You are looking good. I got a quick glimpse of that stud muffin writer from

L.A during the press conference. Your boss sure likes the limelight.

I have good news: I passed the bar exam! My dad is so happy! And I can't wait to go to work full time. Don't get me wrong now. I love my little rug rats. But honey, I need to get on with my plans, you know what I mean. If Jack Danger had his way, I'd be knocked up again in a wink and I'll never get out of here!"

"Oh TJ, I'm so happy for you! That's the best news I've had all day."

"Have you heard from Brian?" TJ was afraid to ask. She knew what the answer would be.

"No. Not a word. Not even a postcard. I know he's married to the Marine Corps. I don't think he even remembers he has a wife. I think I'm over that whole 'I miss my husband' shit."

"Well Darlin', I tried to tell you a long time ago. Your whole marriage was just one of those things you did in life more for obligation than anything else. You just hadn't gotten to the place in your life where you are now. Your nose is out of the books and you are looking at the world around you. And it's about time. You're just coming into your own...as they say here in the South. Me too, really. I had my babies and now it's time for me to pick up my dreams where they left off. So, not to change the subject, but how are things going with Mr. Hollywood? Do you think he's interested? Are *you* interested?"

Julie hesitated for a moment. But she figured if there was one person in her life that knew all of her deepest thoughts, it was TJ. She knew her better than she knew herself. She had always been the voice of reason and her sounding board.

"I don't know what's going on with him. My hands get sweaty and my heart pounds just being near him! I try to not pay attention, but damn, he makes it so hard! And you should smell this man! He's intoxicating!"

"I know what you mean," said TJ. "Jack has a smell about him that makes me crazy! Just like my babies do. You know…it must just be one of those innate things. Like a Mother Nature thing. You smell 'em and you just know they are yours!"

"The weird thing is, that I thought I was picking up some vibes from him that led me to think he was interested in more than just a working relationship. He's always being so attentive and charming. But today, when we got back to the office after the courthouse, he got out of the car and said he was going to L.A. and wouldn't be back until later in the week. He walked over to his car and didn't even look back once. I don't know what to think."

"Well Darlin', you haven't really been giving him any reason to continue to peruse you if you haven't reacted to him. Does he know you are married?"

"No. We haven't had any conversations that would lead me to tell him that. But I will tell him when the time is right. If it ever gets to that point."

"Well, I've always believe in honesty up front. You don't want to start a new relationship without presenting all of the evidence in advance. Ha! Do I sound like a lawyer or what?"

Both of them laughed and finished talking with just general conversation. But after they hung up, Julie soaked for a long time. It was her place to think. There was something about the water that just relaxed her mind and she could always think better. She wondered what Alex had left for. She decided to just let things happen and see if there was anything really there or not. She would open her heart, but with caution. She had no interest in getting her heart broken. After all, her husband was doing a pretty good job of that all on his own.

Around nine that evening, her phone rang. It was Bernie. "Hello there, young lady. Sorry about the late call, but my wife and I have a horse running this Saturday at the Del Mar race track. She's been dying to meet you. We've got a VIP box at the Saddle Club there and we'd like to have you join us. You've been working so hard, we'd like to treat you to a day of relaxation. Now, I won't take no for an answer. It's always a lot of fun. Just you be there by noon. I'll have Ms. Parker put the instructions on your desk. It'll have directions and such."

"Bernie, I don't know what to say. I've never been to the track before. Thank you. I was planning on working through the weekend."

"Nonsense! I won't have it. You be there, young lady. You just be there. Horse's name is 'Not Guilty.' You can be our lucky charm. I'm going to be away from the office for a couple of days. So I'll just see you there. Good luck with the investigator. I know you are meeting him in the morning. I have confidence in you. Take care now."

Julie hung up the phone and felt like a tornado had just run through her home. Bernie was always quick to demand and get what he wanted. She didn't know what to think. She was never one to go out much. She didn't even know what to wear. Already she was feeling nervous and out of place. The Saddle Club. That was probably one of those fancy exclusive parts of the race track for rich people. *Oh well*, she thought. *I'll worry about it tomorrow.* She crawled into bed and was asleep before her head hit the pillow. It had been a very long day and she was exhausted.

When morning came, she sped off to the office for that nine o'clock meeting with the detective. When she walked in, she couldn't help but look at the cubicle next to hers. Alex was missing and she felt his absence. He had only been there a short while, and the atmosphere wasn't the same in the office. Trying not to think about it, she put her briefcase down. As she did, she noticed a small bud vase on her desk with some azaleas. There was a note: "Try not to miss me too much. Alex."

Instantly, a smile came over her face. She sat down and read it again. She reached out to smell the flowers and touch them to her cheek. Just about that time, Ms. Parker walked up to her desk. When Julie noticed her standing there, she saw her staring at the bud vase and at her with a very displeasing look on her face. She placed an envelope on her desk.

"Mr. Rosenthal asked that I give this to you." With that, she noticed Ms. Parker reading the note in her hands. She gave Julie disapproving nod and walked away. Julie didn't care.

She was happy now. Today was going to be a good day. He *was* interested.

After her long meeting with the investigator, Julie decided she would go sit in Central Park and read. She liked going there during her lunch hour, and hadn't taken the time in a long while to just do it. There was a large oak tree near the fountain that had a picnic table she always liked to sit on just to unwind. She walked the two short blocks to her spot, took out a book she had started months ago, and began to read and eat an apple. It was such a lovely day and she had so much distracting her that she finally put the book down and began to look around. She was still worried about what to wear to the horse races, and wondering why Alex had left the island. She remembered what TJ had told her the night before. Right as always, her friend had pointed out that she'd been so busy working to become a lawyer that she hadn't really begun to look at her life and what she really wanted. It was such a peaceful place, and her heart was feeling so light today.

Julie just sat there listening to the birds and smelling the flowers and the trees. She felt as if things were about to change for her. Something inside of her told her it was okay to just let go and let it be. She couldn't help but smile on her walk back to the office.

Chapter 10

Saturday morning, Julie was awakened by the door-bell. She looked at her alarm clock and saw that it was eight in the morning. Half asleep, she threw on her bathrobe and stumbled over to open the door.

"Hi Sunshine! I brought doughnut holes!"

"Alex? What are you doing here? How did you get my address?"

"Can I come in? Will you make us some coffee? Or would you like me to do it? You look like you could use coffee."

Julie unlatched the screen door and opened it. Alex stepped inside and looked around. "Nice place. Did you decorate it yourself?"

"Yes, and how did you get my address? When did you get back?"

"Oh, I got into town last night around ten. Where is your kitchen?" Alex began to walk through the living room and entered the kitchen with Julie right behind him. "Where is your coffee pot?"

"Just sit down. I'll make the coffee." Alex took a seat at the kitchen table and watched Julie intently as she made the coffee. Her robe was shear, and he was enjoying watching the contour of her body through the soft, light-pink, silky material.

"I came to pick you up. Bernie has invited me to the track. He mentioned that you were coming, so I told him I'd pick you up and make sure you went. He was very adamant that you come. His wife really wants to meet you. He gave me your address."

"Oh, I had no idea you were invited as well. I don't even know what to wear. I've never been to the track. And they have a private box at the Saddle Club. Isn't that for all of the ritzy people?"

Julie poured the coffee and placed two cups at the table. She sat down as Alex opened the familiar small white bag of doughnut holes and began to dunk one into his cup. Julie realized he was sitting on the side of the table where Brian had pounded her when he'd been home last Thanksgiving. Sitting across from Alex, she gave herself permission to really look into his eyes, and that thought instantly left her mind. He had the most amazing green eyes. They seemed to smile all by themselves. His sandy blonde hair softly covered just the tip of his ears. She almost wanted to reach across and fix it. He really was incredibly handsome.

"I wouldn't worry too much about the ritzy people. You'll fit right in. With your charm and great looks, it won't matter what you wear. We really should be there by noon or we'll miss the running of his horse. I'll come back and pick you up. What time should I be here?"

Julie slurped her coffee a little as she took a bite of the doughnut hole she had dunked. "I guess around ten-thirty? It shouldn't take more than an hour to get to Del Mar, don't you think?"

Alex reached over and softly wiped the coffee from Julie's chin with his finger. His touch filled her with excitement. She smiled at him and he smiled back. There was definitely a connection there. She felt her heart pound in her chest.

Alex looked at Julie with a half-smile. He was feeling it too. He examined her face and loved her pale complexion and rosy cheeks. Even with no makeup, this woman was beautiful.

When they had finished making small talk and eaten all of the doughnut holes, Julie told him to get out so she could have time to get ready. As they walked toward the door, Alex spotted a photo on the bookshelf. It was an eight-by-ten frame with Julie's and Brian's wedding photo. He stopped dead in his tracks and picked it up and began to examine it. His mouth dropped open and he felt his heart sink.

"Who is this Marine in the picture? Are you married?"

Suddenly, Julie saw Alex's face change. There was a pale look about him, and his cheery personality was gone.

"That is my husband, Brian. He's away somewhere in the Middle East. He's involved in the war."

"I didn't realize you were married. You don't wear a ring. No one told me."

"I'm pretty private at work. I don't like to mix work with my personal life, what there is of it.

My ring slipped down the drain. I just haven't had a chance to replace it. I'm sorry you didn't know, but you never really asked."

"No, I guess I didn't." Alex placed the photo back on top of the bookshelf and opened the door. He looked at Julie and said. "I'll be back to get you later." He walked out and closed the door behind him. Julie felt terrible. He looked as if the air had been let out of him. Her heart sank too. She hadn't really betrayed him. There just hadn't been an occasion to have the discussion about her marital status. She couldn't blame herself. He had come on to her without questioning. But it didn't make her feel any better. *"Oh well,"* she thought. *It's just as well it's all out in the open*. Now there would be no games. No more wondering if he was attracted to her. There was no chance of anything happening between them now.

Julie went into her closet and looked for something appropriate to put on. She decided on a flower print summer dress and a matching sweater. She took a quick shower and dried her hair. She decided to leave it down. Always having to look professional, she never got a chance to do that. She decided to go a little heavier on the makeup being that she wasn't going to work, and didn't mind a little more eye shadow and rouge. She glided her lip gloss on her lips and before too long, the doorbell rang again. Alex had come back to fetch her. She opened the door and walked out. He was wearing a cream-colored suit and a light lavender shirt. He looked amazing.

"You look very nice. You'll fit right in with all those ritzy people," he said to her with a forced smile. Julie could tell his demeanor toward her had already changed. He opened the car door and she slid in. He had left the top down on his convertible and she didn't mind. It was a really lovely day and she was excited to have some place to go.

"Is it okay if I leave the top down?" he asked. "I can put it up if the wind gets to be too much for you."

"No, it's fine. I've never ridden in a convertible before. It looks like fun."

"Well then, off we go, Mrs. Turner."

And there it was. The first jab. Now she knew he wasn't going to be responding to her as before. He would now hold her at arm's length and their relationship would simply be a professional one. Julie felt sad about that. But she also felt a relief that it was all out in the open. She tried to sit back, relax, and just enjoy the day.

They drove to the Del Mar race track in almost silence. Alex had a nice music tape playing in his car. She was enjoying his music, and that gave them a reason not to have to speak to one another.

When they arrived, he showed the parking attendant a pass, and they were directed to an area where they had valet parking. One of the men opened the door for Julie and Alex handed the keys to another one. They pointed them to a set of stairs that led to an elevator. The man inside rode them to the top floor where the private club was.

Once inside, there was another man who walked them over to the suite where the Rosenthal's were, as well their son, who was also a partner. He was there with his wife. There were also several older gentlemen and ladies, all sitting around talking and drinking.

"Come on in!" exclaimed Bernie when he saw them arrive. Mrs. Rosenthal stood up and walked up to Alex to give him a kiss on the cheek.

"So happy to see you again, Alex. I'm so excited you're working with Bernie on his little book project. And you must be Julie. I'm so happy to finally meet you. Bernie brags about you all the time. He says you are the brightest young lawyer he's ever met. He has big plans for you, you know?"

"Why, thank you Mrs. Rosenthal. It is a pleasure to meet you as well."

"Now, you must call me Sylvia. I'm only Mrs. Rosenthal to strangers. I already feel like I know you. Come sit down by me. Bernie, get these two young people something to drink. Alex, how is your father getting along. I heard he wasn't well?"

"Actually, I was out to see them this week. He's doing much better. Thank you for asking."

Julie heard this and realized that's where Alex must have been earlier in the week. Mrs. Rosenthal was a tall, charming, silver-haired lady who was a bit on the chubby side. She was impeccably dressed in a pink linen dress and matching shoes. Her hair was in a loose bun in the back of her head, and she sported a double strand of pearls around her neck that reminded her of First Lady Mrs. Bush. Bernie returned with martinis for the two, and began introducing them to the other people in the room. There were a couple of old judges he knew from his days in law school and their wives.

"I'd like to make a toast. Let's drink to Not Guilty. May he leave them in the dust."

With that, they all raised and clinked their glasses.

"Well, I think I'd better go place my bet," said Alex. "Please excuse me. Would you like me to place a bet for you, too?" he said, looking at Julie.

"Sure, why not? Here, let me give you some money."

"No, don't worry about it. This one is on me." Julie watched as he walked away toward the back of the room. She was still feeling guilty about the incident this morning. She really didn't know what was running through his mind, and that bothered her.

Julie sat back and watched the others continue with their conversations. She decided to walk over to the large window and get a good look at the track. It was beautiful. As she watched the race that was in progress, she was also looking around at the spectacular view. She could even see the ocean at a distance. It looked exciting. Alex came up to stand next to her and they watched the race. He brought Julie another drink.

"You don't seem like a martini kind of person. Here's a piña colada."

"Thank you. I've never been much of a drinker. This looks delicious." Julie took a sip and licked her lips. "Mmmm, this is good. Thanks. I could get used to these."

"Take it easy. Too many of those and I'll have to drive you home in my trunk." Alex clinked his glass to hers and took a sip. "If you look on top of that hill up there, you'll be able to see the home that belonged to the old actor Jimmie Durante. He loved this track so much, he had it built so he could watch the races from that huge glass window up there. He used to throw parties all the time and invite other famous actors like Bob Hope and Bing Crosby. They all loved this place."

He paused for a moment and Julie took the opportunity to speak up. "Alex, I feel really bad about earlier today. I had no intention of deceiving you in any way."

"Don't feel bad. I had no right to just assume anything. I mean, we don't really know each other. We'll talk about it some other time. Maybe you'll give me that opportunity to buy you dinner some time and we can get to know each other better. I think you're terrific. He's a very lucky man, your husband. Let's just enjoy the day."

"Here we go!" shouted Bernie. This is our race!" They opened the sliding door to the box and everyone walked outside onto the porch to watch the race. Bernie and Sylvia couldn't stand still from the excitement. They watched the horses' parade by and walk over to the gate. 'Not Guilty' was a spectacular thoroughbred. He was chestnut-colored with a large white spot on his face. He strutted past everyone with all the confidence of a winner. Once all of the horses were inside the gate, they rang the bell and all of them raced by, leaving a big cloud of dust behind them. The announcer called the race as it progressed. Not Guilty was third from the end. After the first turn, he made his way to the inside and ran like his butt was on fire. Everyone in the stands was on their feet and they were all shouting. Bernie and Sylvia were jumping up and down. He ran faster and made his way up to the front. He was neck in neck with a black horse that was called 'To Die For.' Then, once they got to the last stretch, he sped up and left 'To Die For' in the dust, winning the race by a length.

Bernie and Sylvia were ecstatic, hugging everyone as they made their way towards the winner's circle. Julie thought it was a lot of fun watching Bernie outside of his usual serious lawyer persona. He was obviously a very kind and happy person. After all, he had done a lot for Julie, and she was very grateful that he had taken her under his wing.

Toward the end of the afternoon, everyone was settled back down in their comfortably stuffed chairs, just visiting with one another. Sylvia had been watching the interaction between Alex and Julie and finally said. "You know, you two make a lovely pair. I think I see a romance brewing."

Julie turned bright red. Alex just smiled.

"Oh Sylvia, you are always up to something. I wouldn't hold my breath if I were you. This lovely lady has much better taste than to pick someone like me. I think it's getting to be around that time. Shall I get you home?"

Sylvia looked at the two of them and said. "Oh, I'm rarely wrong about these things. You can run, but you can't hide from me. Just you wait and see, my friend. May I see your left hand please, Julie?"

Julie obliged her and extended her hand, which she turned upside down. Sylvia began to run her index finger up and down the palm lines on Julie's hand. She closed her eyes for a moment and smiled. She then closed Julie's hand, smiled, and let it go.

"Julie, it was so nice to meet you. Thank you for helping Bernie. He's not getting any younger. I wish he'd retire soon. I want to travel before we get too old to walk. Don't be strangers, you two. Alex, you give your parents a hug from me when you see them next, please."

"I shall." Alex gave Sylvia a hug. He extended his hand to Julie and helped her to stand. They bid their good-byes to all and thanked Bernie for a wonderful afternoon.

Chapter 11

As they drove back to Coronado Island, they had the music blasting and the wind blew Julie's hair. She put her head back onto the head rest and closed her eyes. She was enjoying the ride. It was very freeing to her being in an open convertible. It was just dusk when they began to cross the bridge.

"It's been such a perfect day," said Julie. "Thank you for taking me."

"It really is a great sunset, and the day's been pretty great. You know, I really enjoy your company. I'd really like to take you to dinner. What do you say? I'm not sure I want this day to end quite yet."

"Well, a girl's got to eat. Why not? Let's go grab a bite somewhere. What kind of food do you like?"

"Why don't you just let me pick the place? I think you'll like it."

Julie looked at Alex and said, "I hope I don't regret this, but okay. You pick."

Alex got off the bridge and turned up Central Avenue. When he got almost to the end of the island, he turned in to the Hotel Del Coronado, a majestic old resort hotel that was built in 1888. Its grand white walls and red roof made it stand out from the rest of the island.

"Alex, this place is expensive. Why don't we go somewhere else?" protested Julie.

"Aww, come on. We only get to have our first dinner once. Let's make it one to remember."

Alex pulled the car right up to the front door and the valets came to take his keys. As he walked to Julie's side of the car, he took her hand to help her up the stairs. Julie felt that current again. Like the time he shook her hand for the first time. His touch stirred her, even just the touching of their hands. This made her nervous again. It was a great feeling. They walked hand in hand through the hotel, toward the back. He seemed to know where he was going, so she just let him lead her. He took her out the back glass doors and to a huge outdoor patio that had big fire pits and tables.

Alex led Julie to a table and held her chair out for her, then he sat right next to her. The sun was just about to touch the horizon, and the colors of the evening were spectacular.

"What a magnificent place!" she said, looking at him. "I've never been here before. I guess I never get out much."

A waiter came over and Alex ordered a bottle of champagne and several hors d'oeurves. Julie liked the 'take charge' way in which he just took over ordering for her. She thought it was very sexy. He was obviously someone who had been around the block a time or two. She hadn't really ever dated anyone but Brian, and he never took her anyplace. This was a new experience for her, and she realized how much she was missing in her life.

"Look at the colors of the sky. I've never seen a more colorful sunset. Thanks for having dinner with me. I walked around this place the first week I got here and I've been dying to have an excuse to come back. I can't think of a better person to come for the experience with than you."

The waiter returned and poured the champagne. Alex lifted his glass and said, "To the beginning of a new and wonderful friendship."

Julie found herself looking deep into Alex's eyes again. He stared at her as she looked at him and asked, "Is something wrong? Is this okay?"

Julie's eyes began to well up with tears. He looked at her with a worried look and reached out to dab them with his cloth napkin. "I've done something you don't approve of, haven't I? I can order something else if you don't like champagne?"

"No, you haven't done anything wrong. It's just that this is all new to me. I don't know why I'm going to tell you all of this, I don't even know you. I'm very unhappy in my marriage. I don't even know what I'm even doing married to Brian. I think it's just an obligation or a feeling of duty."

Julie began to tell Alex the whole story. They sat and drank the champagne and ate some food. He just listened. As he did, he realized she had a lot bottled up inside of her. By the time the two hours had passed, he felt as if he knew her even better than her own husband. This was a beautiful, intelligent woman who had never experienced real love in her life. She had been used and ignored. She'd never experienced the real romantic passionate kind of love that every woman deserves. She wasn't being held, or touched. She was merely existing in a relationship of convenience.

Alex began to tell Julie of his experiences in love as well. He shared with her his heartbreak this past November when he'd come home early from an assignment for the TV station he worked for. He told her that when he walked in the door to his apartment, he heard noises. And when he walked into his bedroom, he found his live-in girlfriend riding his best friend and colleague from work. He'd recently found out she was pregnant with that man's baby. He'd wanted to settle down and have a family, but she kept putting him off. Seemingly, he hadn't been the right guy for her and she'd never had the guts to tell him. She had just led him on until something better came along.

The two of them talked for what seemed like hours before the waiter brought the check. They'd been enjoying sitting outside on the patio near the tiki torches and fire pit. Alex paid the bill and suggested they take a walk on the beach. The air was on the cool side, and the breeze was light.

The two of them took off their shoes and walked in the sand in the direction of Point Lobos. They didn't say much. They just listened to the waves break and looked at the star-filled sky. The powder-soft sand felt cool on the bottom of their feet. The smell of the salty air was refreshing. At a distance, they could hear a band from one of the hotel clubs playing.

Julie said to Alex, "I think I'm just going to sit down and make a list of all the things I haven't done with my life and want to get started doing. Like someday, I want to dance in the moonlight."

Alex looked at Julie and said, "Why someday? Why not tonight? I've never danced in the moonlight either." He stepped back, offered her his hand and said, "May I have this first moonlight dance?"

Julie laughed nervously and took his hand. Before she knew it, he had drawn her into his arms. He was holding her close and it took her breath away. She could feel his cool hand on the small of her back. The chemistry between them was electrifying, and the attraction was amazing. Alex buried his head in her hair. He loved the way she smelled. She felt perfect in his arms. Their hands were clutched and they felt as if they were welded together into one. They swayed with the music and Alex began to sing along softly with the song that they heard playing. Julie felt as if she was watching it all in a dream. This was so surreal, she'd never felt like this.

"*Can't smile without you…..can't smile without you…*" He sang to her as they continued to dance. "Do you like Manilow?" he asked.

"Who?" she asked.

"Barry Manilow. That's his song they are playing. He's great in concert."

"I've never been to a concert," she said. "I guess I'd better put that on my list, too."

"Well then, I shall take you. I think he's coming to L.A. soon."

Julie was enjoying being in Alex's arms so much she didn't want the evening to end. She could feel him between them. He was fully erect and was pressing on her at just the right spot. She began to feel hot and was finding it hard to resist tearing his clothes off and just making love to him right there on the spot. They had made a connection tonight. And she didn't know if it was a good thing or a bad thing. All she knew was that if she could stop time, she would stop it right now.

Alex was finding it very difficult not to kiss Julie. He wanted to so badly. She had excited him and he didn't want to lose it. But he knew he had to be a gentleman. After all, she was married and he didn't know where this would lead. He hoped it would be somewhere wonderful.

"I think I'd better get you home now. It's getting late." Alex took Julie by the hand and they walked toward the car. As they drove toward her house, she quietly looked at him. She knew she wanted this man. But tonight wasn't the right time.

Alex walked Julie to her door. As she was about to go inside, he placed his hand on her face to draw her near him and kissed her on the cheek. "Now what? Where do we go from here?"

Julie didn't respond. She didn't have an answer. She just said, "Good night Alex. Thank you."

Once inside, she looked at the clock and saw it read midnight. It was too late to call TJ, but she wished she could. She had so many feelings stirring up her insides. So many questions she needed help answering. There was no way she would get to sleep any time soon. She threw off her clothes, put on a bathrobe and made herself a cup of tea. She decided to take it outside onto the front porch and crawl onto a patio chair. Looking at the sky, she just wanted to try to make sense of what had just happened. Not once, ever, had she had a day or night like this one.

What do I do? She asked the stars. *Should I let this happen? Should I just forget about this intense feeling I have for this man? I want him. I want him so badly.* She questioned everything she ever thought to be real and true. At that moment, she was lost in her conflict. Married and not having any feelings for her husband, and wanting to pursue a happiness she had never known. She wondered if she deserved it.

When morning came, she was awakened by the telephone. Half asleep, she lifted up the receiver only to hear TJ on the other end.

"Well, don't keep me in suspense! How was your day at the track?" she asked.

"Oh TJ, I wish you were here. I need to just sit and tell you everything that has happened. I don't know where to begin...."

TJ just listened to her friend as she cried and re-lived the whole day from start to finish. From the whole terrible way Alex found out she was married, to the dance on the beach, and the kiss at the front door. Julie talked and TJ listened for almost an hour before she was able to get a word in. But she knew her friend just needed to dump everything she was holding inside. She knew her friend was in pain.

The deep, terrible pain that only comes with heartbreak and confusion.

"Girlfriend, I tried to tell you he'd be the one. Now you know that when the man is the right man, you'll walk on hot coals just to be with him. You just need to tell Brian as soon as he gets back that you want out. That marriage should have never have happened. You've seen how Jack Danger and I have been droolin' all over each other since we met. If your man is the right man, it never goes away. The desire and love is always going to be there."

Julie listened and told TJ she was afraid of hurting Brian and disappointing their families.

"So, you'd rather be miserable the rest of your life and lose the one chance you might have at finding the right kind of love, just so you don't hurt and disappoint other people? Do you want me to come out there and shake you? Snap out of it! You know I'll get on a plane! Let it be. Go with it. Find out if this is what you want. You have nothing to lose and you'll have a great time and you'll get to experience things you've never had the opportunity to experience. God didn't put this man in your path for no reason. There has to be a reason."

Julie knew she was right, and her advice is just what she needed to hear. TJ always gave her sound words. She was her rock.

After the phone call, she decided to go shopping, something she hardly ever did. There was no food in the house, and her work was caught up. This would give her time to digest the previous day and see how she felt when Monday morning came. It occurred to her that she might hear from Alex, but thought he might be giving her some space. So she didn't look for the phone to ring. And it didn't. The day came and went. She spent it catching up with things at home. But she couldn't wait until Monday.

Chapter 12

The Monday morning meeting started promptly at eight every week. Bernie used it to catch up with all of the partners and their associates regarding new clients and cases that they were working on, and they would determine the amount of billable hours they had turned in. After all, the practice was just like any other business. They needed to make money to stay in business.

Everyone filed into the large conference room upstairs. Ms. Parker always had fruit and pastries and four pots of coffee down the center of the table for everyone. Bernie started by going around the room asking each and every attorney in the firm for an update on their work.

Ms. Parker took notes, still in shorthand, and then recorded them as part of the company record book. This helped the CPAs also with their financial information about the firm. Julie kept looking at the door to see if Alex was coming. But this meeting didn't really pertain to anything he had been hired to write about. So his absence at the meeting wasn't a surprise. She was anxious to see him, glancing at her watch often. She wondered if he was already downstairs, or if he was going to come in later. After a long hour and a half, the meeting finally adjourned. She was the first one out the door and down the stairs. Alex wasn't at his desk. She took a quick glance around the room and spotted him talking to one of the clerks on the other side of the room. They seemed to be having a long conversation and laughing. Julie got a knot in her stomach. *Could this be jealousy?* She asked herself. Why would seeing him talking to another woman make her feel this way? It had to be jealousy. This was a feeling she wasn't familiar with.

Alex spotted Julie at her desk and walked toward her. "Hello, Sunshine," he said with a big grin. "How was the rest of your weekend?"

"Pretty uneventful. How was yours?"

"Oh, quiet. I took a long walk on the beach and even sat and read a book for a while. Still trying to digest everything. Are you free for lunch?"

Julie sat and looked at her schedule book. "I don't know yet. Bernie told us that the judge on the school teacher case has ordered the trial date for next Monday. That doesn't give us too much more time to prepare. I'll have to let you know."

"Monday, huh? Well, that's exciting. I guess I'd better get in there and talk to Bernie and get a game plan going. By the way, there is something under your mug you might want to take a look at." Alex turned and walked away in the direction of Bernie's office. He stopped to chat with Ms. Parker for a moment before going in.

Julie looked at her mug. Underneath, there was a white envelope. She reached for it, and on the front it said: 'Please come with me.' She looked inside and pulled out two concert tickets. They were for the upcoming Saturday night. 'The Greek Theater, Barry Manilow,' 8:00 PM. Her mouth dropped open. She didn't know what to think. Julie looked in the direction of Bernie's office. Alex was standing inside with his arms crossed, waiting for him to get off the phone. He saw Julie's reaction. It was what he was hoping for. He smiled and winked at her. She managed a smile back, but she still didn't know what to say or what to think. She was excited and scared at the same time. She'd never been to a concert anywhere, and now she'd been invited to go with him. Of course she was going. She was going to take the advice TJ had given her and just relax and enjoy whatever came along. How thoughtful he was. He didn't forget that she mentioned not ever having attended a live concert. This was a very special man. She wondered why she had thought him to be such an arrogant pain in the butt when she had first met him. It must have been her misunderstanding her attraction to him.

Julie's phone rang. It was the investigator. He wanted to meet with her in the afternoon to discuss what he'd found. Good thing, too. Now that the judge had set the court date, things had to be moving along very quickly. She set the meeting for two o'clock.

When Alex returned, she told him about the meeting and that lunch was out of the question.

"That's all right, Sunshine. I have to go to the jail with Bernie. He's going to visit with the school teacher and fill her in with what will be happening next week. I'd better go along.

I'm going to have to document most of what's going on. I guess we'll make it some other time."

"Sure, I have to meet with the investigator this afternoon. So, I won't be going to the jail with him this time. I'm sure he can handle it," she said with a smile.

After the meeting with the detective was over, Julie decided to take a break from the office. She'd been locked up all day getting as much pretrial stuff done as possible. She decided to take a walk down to the park and just sit for a few minutes and get some fresh air. The two short walks would do her good. It would give her a stretch. She was starting to get stiff sitting for so long. She grabbed one of the leftover apples from the morning meeting and took it with her. When she got to the park, she sat on the table under the tree she loved so much near the fountain. Just sitting there listening to the birds, and the breeze helped her to relax. She ate her apple and closed her eyes. She couldn't get Saturday night out of her mind. Just thinking about Alex and the way she felt when he was holding her dancing excited her. She liked the feeling that came over her when she pictured herself in his arms. *The concert should be exciting too,* she thought to herself. She couldn't wait to go. As she sat there with her eyes closed, she heard a voice.

"Hi, Sunshine. Want some company?" Alex had found her. He was standing right in front of her.

"Are you stalking me, sir?" she asked with a smile. "How did you find me?"

"I thought I saw you when Bernie and I drove by. I thought I was going to die in that big Mercedes of his. He drives like an old man on a mission. What are you doing here all by yourself?"

"I come here all the time. It's my refuge when I need time alone to think or just to unwind. It's a close walk from the office. How long have you been standing there?"

Alex sat down across from Julie. "Long enough to see how beautiful you look in the afternoon sunlight. You are beautiful, you know?"

Julie began to turn red and looked down. "I'm not. I'm just an ordinary thing."

"Hardly. And you really should learn to take a compliment. When someone tells you that you're beautiful, you should just learn to say 'thank you.'"

"It's just that aside from my mom, I've never been told things like that before."

"That's a shame. You should get used to it."

Julie examined Alex's smile. She knew he meant what he said. Brian never paid her any compliments. At least, not for years. It was hard for her to accept remarks like that about herself.

"How did it go at the jail? How is she holding up? I'm sure Bernie had a bunch of questions for her and gave her the right act about next Monday."

"Well, I know people are supposed to be considered not guilty until proven otherwise. But in my personal opinion, that is one narcissistic crazy woman. She is so full of herself! And it's okay that it's my opinion. I'm not her lawyer. But she is one piece of work that one. I think she really believes she's going to walk. Bernie was up front with her. He told her all of the evidence was stacked against her and that he'd do what he could to keep her off of the electric chair. But he was honest and right flat out said she'd better prepare herself for a long visit to a not-so-glamorous resort compliments of the state of California. Can I walk you back to the office?"

"I don't think that's a good idea. We shouldn't really be seen together unless its work related. I'm already getting 'the look' from Ms. Parker."

"Gotcha. Well, how about coming to my place for dinner tonight? I make a mean spaghetti."

"Well, if you're going to twist my arm. I probably won't be out of here until late. Is that okay?"

"That's fine. I'm going to go home and do some work on the book. I'll just throw the sauce in and let it simmer until you get there. We can watch TV or something. Don't bring anything. Just yourself."

"Great. I love spaghetti. I'm going to go now."

"My car is right over there. I'll see you later, Sunshine."

Alex stood up and extended his hand to Julie. As he helped her up, he pulled her close to him. She could smell that cologne. The touch of his hand and the smell of him made her legs weak. He kissed her on the cheek again, and she felt herself getting wet. Every time this man comes close to her, she feels like a leaky faucet.

Julie finished out her day and went home to wash up and change. She sure wasn't going to his house in a business suit that she'd worn all day. She checked her mail, and was not surprised. There was no letter from Brian. There was never anything from Brian. But she was over that. She was just going to focus on what she wanted now, and she would deal with ending things with him when he got home.

Julie decided to call TJ and catch her up to things. She caught her right after her first full day as an official practicing lawyer. Her dad and brother had made her a partner, but that was to be expected. She knew it would become official when she started work.

"Hey! I had such a good day today! I got to be away from all my little men for ten whole hours! Imagine that? Not an ounce of testosterone in my office all day! Just a decorator and interviewing for an assistant. It was a glorious day for me! So tell me, what's going on with Mr. Hollywood? Are you going to nail him or what?"

"TJ, I can always count on you to be direct and say what's on your mind. I do have some things to tell you. He is taking me to a Manilow concert on Saturday, and he is fixing me spaghetti tonight at his place."

"Like my Granny used to say, 'Jesus take the wheel'! Child, I hope you aren't planning on wearing your old granny panties over to his house. Do you even own a G-string?"

"I don't even know what that is. And I don't intend on him seeing my panties. Why? What's wrong with my panties?"

"Girl, if you are still using the same ones you did when we were in college, you'd better get some shopping in before you start bedding this man. He'll wonder if you live in the dark ages. I'll go online tonight and order you some of Jack Danger's favorite ones. I'll overnight you some. Don't you let him see you naked in those old giant white things! He'll never go back for seconds! And you'd better call me after the concert and fill me in on all the dirty details. I'll be waiting."

"Okay, okay. And congratulations on finally getting to work. You go get'm."

Chapter 13

*J*ulie was now self-conscious about what to wear. TJ had scared her half to death about her clothes. She'd never had cause to worry about styles or the latest fashions. When she bought business suits, she would go to one of the large department stores where they had personal shoppers and let them help her. But that was totally different than casual clothes. At home, she lived in sweatpants or her bathrobe. She'd never really given lingerie a second thought. Brian hadn't expressed any interest in it, and she'd always been too shy to walk into one of those stores at the mall to see what was in there. But if she was going to make a change, that was something else she would put on her list of new things to try. Right now, she was just trying to find something to put on that didn't make her look too frumpy to eat spaghetti in. She settled on just a pair of jeans and a blue tank top.

It was eight o'clock when she arrived at Alex's cottage. He greeted her at the door and gave her a hug. "Welcome to Casa Hart."

"Alex, that smell is amazing. Did you make that sauce yourself? I've never had a man cook for me before. Except my dad. He kills it on the barbecue."

Julie looked around and said with a wink, "I love what you've done with the place. All the flowered wall paper is definitely you." She walked into the kitchen and asked, "May I have a taste?"

"Sure, I made it just for you." He lifted the lid and gave her a small teaspoon to taste.

"Oh Alex, this is wonderful! Your mom raised you right."

"Come sit at the table. I'll get us some wine." Alex pulled the chair out away from the small round table in the little eating area and began to uncork the bottle. Julie looked around and couldn't help but smile. He had obviously gone through some trouble for her. The fireplace was lit. There were candles lit everywhere, and there were fresh cut flowers from the garden in small vases on the table and all around the room. Soft jazzy music played in the background. When he returned with the wine, he offered a toast.

"To the Italians, for inventing such an easy meal to prepare." They clinked their glasses.

Julie took a sip and laughed. She found Alex very witty. Sitting in his home being waited on hand and foot, was not something she was accustomed to. In fact, it was something she had never experienced. Another thing she realized she'd never had. It felt quite nice.

Alex plated the salad and the spaghetti and put it on the table. She could see the steam coming off the hot pasta, and everything looked delicious.

"I hope you enjoy it. I cooked to impress," Alex said as he sat down next to her.

"Spaghetti? Is that your signature dish?"

"Well, no. Actually I can *shmear* the heck out of cream cheese on bagels. But that's another meal," he said laughingly.

Julie began to eat. She must have been really hungry because everything tasted great. "I can't remember when I had my last home-cooked meal. I usually just open a can of soup or something."

"Here, let me show you the method to my madness. Spaghetti is a very romantic meal, you know?" He twirled a piece of pasta on his fork and placed one end of it on Julie's lips. "Grab this," he said, and he put the other end between his lips. "Now, start eating. I bought the extra-long pasta just for this experiment." They both laughed as they began eating and slurping the long strand of spaghetti. Their lips were just a mere inch away from touching. Alex looked into Julie's eyes. He could see the candlelight bouncing off of them and he felt himself stirring below. They paused for what seemed an eternity. Julie was looking back at him. He moved his face close to hers and took the last little piece of the spaghetti while giving her a soft kiss, his lips barely touching hers.

"I don't know what tastes better. You or my pasta. I'm going to have to have another taste test." He slowly moved his lips toward hers again. This time, he paused for a second before touching them tenderly, slowly. As he kissed her, Julie was once again stirred by the strong chemistry between them. She wished she'd listened to TJ and not worn her usual panties.

"Thank you," said Alex. "That was delicious. Let me pour you more wine so we can finish our meal."

Julie felt like he was taunting her. He was taunting her with just little bits and pieces of himself, making her want more. And she wanted more. He was obviously taking it slow, giving her the opportunity to say no if she felt she needed to. But what he didn't know was that she had made up her mind. She was all in. She wanted it all.

After they finished eating, Alex suggested they go up to Orange Street to buy ice cream. He hadn't had time to pick some up on the way home. It was such a nice night, they walked up to the old-fashioned ice cream store. Alex ordered two chocolate sugar cones. As they were at the door about to leave, Ms. Parker walked in with her nephews. She looked quite surprised to see the two of them out together away from work.

"Ms. Parker, isn't it a nice evening?" said Alex.

She only glared at them and answered, "Well, it's an interesting evening for sure."

They walked out the door as quickly as they could, and when they got outside, they laughed out loud. "Well, we're busted aren't we?" laughed Alex. When they crossed Orange and were on their way down Isabella Street, Alex took Julie's hand. They walked together back toward his cottage and took turns licking each other's ice creams, laughing and pondering at the horrors of Ms. Parker's wrath. She obviously did not approve. Julie felt special when he took her hand. She felt as if they belonged together. It was so natural.

Once back inside, Alex put another log on the fire and sat on the couch next to Julie. They didn't speak. The soft music was the only sound. That, and Julie's heart pounding. The connection told it all. Alex put his arm around Julie and she slid up against him. "Are you nervous?" he asked.

"Why do you ask? Do I seem nervous?"

"I can hear your heart. It's beating so loud. Don't be nervous, Sunshine. Don't be nervous. We'll take it as slow as you say." Alex began to kiss Julie's neck, softly running his tongue up to her ear lobe. She immediately reacted to his touch and turned her face toward his. He used the tip of tongue to brush across her lips slowly. He felt himself arousing as he placed a kiss on her lips. This time, the kiss didn't stop. It lingered without end. Julie was wet. He continued to kiss her and kiss her. As he did, she could feel herself heat up and stir to his touch. She felt her nipples harden like rocks. She'd never been kissed this long before. Alex began to run his hand slowly down the small of Julie's back and up again. After some time, Alex spoke.

"Sunshine, I think you should go home. I want to make sure you to have everything resolved in your head. I know your situation, and as badly as I want you, I'll wait for *you* to decide when the right time is. I don't want us to make any mistakes. You're the one that has to live with it."

Julie was so intoxicated with his kisses, she could hardly speak. "Okay. Thank you for putting me first."

Alex stood and helped Julie up. Her legs felt like the spaghetti they had just eaten. He walked her out to her car, and before she got in, he turned her with her back to the car and pressed himself onto her. He wanted her to feel him. He wanted her to know what she did to him. How ready he was to take her. Julie was hot and soaked with her juices. He turned her on like a faucet. "Good night, Sunshine. See you in the morning."

Julie turned her car on and slowly began to drive away. When she was able to compose herself, she mumbled: *TJ was right. I'd better go shopping!* She giggled to herself.

The next few days were going to be brutal. The district attorney was throwing the book at their client. True, she hadn't been the one to pull the trigger on her husband, but she was the mastermind and an accessory for sure. They were charging her with first-degree murder. She had been the one to supply the boys with the gun. That was their proof of pre-meditation. What was going to really lock her up, were the multiple rape charges against the two minors. They boys had entered a plea after striking a deal. They would get lighter sentences for cooperating and assisting the D.A. in getting her locked up for statutory rape and other charges, such as contributing to the delinquency of minors.

The whole team was going to have to put in some long hours getting the defense in order. Bernie was counting on Julie for that. She really had to focus this week. Her work was crucial to him.

The day following the spaghetti date, Ms. Parker made sure that she and Alex knew, that she knew something was going on. She intentionally gave them dirty looks throughout the day. Julie paid no attention. She had a lot of work to do. She decided to take over the upstairs conference room. The table was large and there was a lot of paperwork. She needed to spread it out to go over all the information with Bernie when he came in. The investigator brought back only negative information on their client. It seems she was known for being a skank of sorts around her husband's co-workers. She'd met him at a bar she frequented to find male companionship. Why she married the guy was unclear. Everyone thought it was because he had come into some money when his mother died and she liked expensive things. He promised he'd buy her a house. After she had gotten what she wanted, she didn't want him around. He had also taken out a large insurance policy and she was counting on spending that when he was out of the way.

Alex knew Julie needed some space this week. He watched as she and Bernie went over the information they were going to use in the trial. Bernie had selected one of the older attorneys in the firm to be second chair at the trial. They knew they were fighting an uphill battle, but they had to do their best for the client. All of the information they had would become part of the book Alex was co-authoring for Bernie, so he was able to sit in on the work being done upstairs. He sat in on all of the meetings, taking notes.

Alex sat back and watched Julie as she worked. He was very impressed with her knowledge of the law, and how good she was at her job. Every morning, he brought her a little white bag with doughnut holes and placed it on her desk. Some days they were too busy to eat lunch, and she was glad to have them. The week was long, as were the days. Not once during that time did anyone on the team go home before ten or eleven. By Friday night, they were ready. Bernie didn't want any work done on that weekend. Everyone was to go home and get some rest. He wanted everyone fresh for the trial on Monday. Julie was grateful for that. She was really looking forward to the concert.

Saturday morning, Alex called Julie at home around nine. "Hey Sunshine, the concert starts at eight. I think we should leave around three. It'll take us two to three hours to get to L.A. depending on traffic. That way we can get an early dinner. The weather isn't looking too good, but the rain isn't predicted to start until late. It should be okay for the concert. Be sure and take a jacket. The Greek Theater is an open air amphitheater and it can get a little chilly. I can't wait to see you."

Julie hung up the phone and panic set in. What to wear? Then, she remembered the package she'd received from TJ earlier in the week. She'd gotten home so late every night, she hadn't had a chance to open it. She put it on the bed and tore into it. Inside, there was a beautiful box with pink tissue paper filled with all kinds of things. There was a note that read: "NO GRANNY PANTIES!" Julie laughed out loud and shook her head. As she began to pull things out, she felt embarrassed. *How was it that I didn't know about this stuff? I must be living in a cocoon.* She said out loud. There were cute little bikini panties and G-strings in every color. She was grateful she hadn't had to go shopping for any of this stuff. She would have died. She pulled out a G-string and tried to figure out how it went on. After a couple of tries, she decided on the bikini panties. They were a bit more comfortable. They were a pretty lilac color, and there was a lacy bra to match. Now all she had to do was figure out what to wear.

She decided to go shopping. She threw on her usual sweat-pants and a top, pulled her hair back with a clip and off to the mall she went. She went into her usual department store and asked for one of the personal shoppers to help her in the ladies department.

"I'm going to an outside concert and I want to look nice," she said to the woman.

"Go in the dressing room and wait. I'll be back in a few minutes." After about ten minutes, the woman came back with all kinds of things draped over her arm. She and Julie looked at several outfits trying them on and mixing and matching. They selected a light gray pant suit with a low cut pink silk shell, giving just a peek of the top of Julie's breasts.

"I'm not sure I can wear this top. I'm showing," she said, examining herself in the mirror. "I don't have anything like this in my wardrobe."

"It's a shame if you don't. You should buy that same shell in different colors. Honey, you have a great figure. Show it off a little. Enjoy your looks while you still have them. Believe me, someday you'll wish you had. Shall I ring these up for you?" she asked.

Julie looked at herself in the mirror again. She remembered that she told herself she was going to do different things. "Sure. And I'll take this top in a couple of different colors, please."

After she got home, she went on a marathon to make herself look extra nice. She showered and curled her hair. She painted her toes, which she never did. She painted her nails, and even shaved her legs, something she rarely had time for. By the time three o'clock rolled around, she took a look in the mirror, smiled at herself and said to herself, *who are you?*

Alex was there precisely on time. She had learned that he had a thing for promptness. She liked that. When she opened the door, his mouth dropped open.

"Wow! You look amazing."

"You look pretty amazing yourself," she said. And he did. He had on a pair of khaki pants, a long-sleeve blue shirt with pin stripes, and a navy blue jacket. He looked hot!

On the way up to Los Angeles, their conversation was light. They always had something to talk about. They discussed the trial, and last week's horse race. Even Ms. Parker came into the conversation. They talked and laughed the entire time. Once in a while, Alex would reach over and squeeze Julie's hand. She loved that. He was so attentive and it felt so good to have someone want to touch her. Even if it was only a squeeze of the hand. Julie had seen her parents do that. After all those years of marriage, they were still in love with each other. They would still laugh and hold hands in public.

"Well, here we are in my town. I know just where I'm going to take you for dinner. You might even see a movie star or two."

As he drove through the city, Julie wondered where they were going. They pulled up in front of a restaurant that had inside and outside seating. The valet came to let Julie out. She looked up and saw the sign. 'The Ivy.' Julie had heard of this place and seen it featured in movies and magazines. She was excited to be somewhere completely out of her norm.

"Table for two," said Alex. The maitre d' led them to a table by a window that overlooked the outside patio. The candles on the table flickered and the lighting was low. There were fresh-cut roses and other flowers on every table.

"This is lovely, Alex. Thank you."

"Oh, it's nothing fancy. But they have really great food here and we're not too far from where we're going and it has great ambiance."

"What's good here?" asked Julie. "I don't know what to order. Everything looks delicious."

"Would you like me to order for you?" asked Alex.

"I'd like that. Anything you like is fine. I don't think I see anything on the menu that I wouldn't eat."

When the waiter returned, he ordered two Mojitos, a house salad, an order of crab cakes, and for each of them, an order of the seafood risotto.

"You don't mind splitting the salad and crab cakes do you? I'm not being cheap, it's just that they are large orders and I don't want to get too full to enjoy the risotto. It's amazing here."

"I don't mind at all. I love just being with you. I'm sure with all that food, I'll be stuffed anyway."

Alex reached across the table and squeezed Julie's hand. He brought it to his face and kissed it. "I love being with you, too. It's making me a little nervous."

"Why? What do you have to be nervous about?

Alex's eyes got a bit watery. She could see them in the candlelight. "I have a feeling I'm going to fall deep and hard, and then you'll kick me to the curb. I don't think I could come back from that. Have I told you how terrific you are?"

"Oh Alex, I don't know what to say. I have very strong feelings for you, too. But you know my situation has to change before I can make any commitments. And it will. But right now I'm at the mercy of the war overseas and the Marine Corps. But I'll handle it the first chance I get."

The waiter returned with the drinks and the salad. They picked at it until the crab cakes came.

"These crab cakes are delicious. I've never had them before."

"You're kidding, right? You live by the ocean and you've never had crab cakes?"

Julie scolded him. "Don't make fun of me. I don't get out much. But I'll make up for lost time. Just you wait and see."

When they finished their dinner, Alex wanted to order dessert. But it was getting late, and Julie protested. She said he was going to have to go borrow a grocery store shopping cart just to get her to the car if she took another bite. So they took a box of the chocolate chip cookies for later.

As they entered Griffith Park and drove up the windy road, Julie noticed the dark grey clouds above them. "Do you think it'll rain on us?"

"It wouldn't dare! Tonight has to be special. It's your first concert." When they arrived, Alex pulled into the VIP parking section of the theater. When they walked in, someone looked at the tickets and showed them to one of the private VIP boxes. They were the only ones there. A photographer came and asked if he could snap a picture. Alex held Julie close and they smiled for the camera.

"Alex, this is too much! You shouldn't have spent so much money. We could have sat anywhere and I would have been happy."

"But I wouldn't have. You deserve your first time to be special. Besides, I know people," he said with a wink.

Julie sat in awe of where she was. Never in a million years would she have ever thought she would be in such a spectacular place. The theater looked just like the one in Greece. All the seats were in stadium-like rows, stepping up higher as they went up from the stage. It was in the middle of the most beautiful canyon she had ever seen. Trees lined the theater all around. There were lights shining up at them. She felt like she was in the middle of a fairy tale. It was chilly and the night sky was covered in clouds. It did look like it was going to rain. But she wasn't going to fret about it. She was just going to enjoy the evening.

A waiter came into the box and asked Alex if he wanted to place a drink order. He asked him to bring two flutes of champagne and a blanket. It wasn't long after that they were snuggling under a blanket, toasting the evening.

Then the announcement came introducing Barry Manilow and the music began blasting. The stage was filled with color and dancers. Then, there he was! Singing as if it were just for them. The whole thing felt so surreal to Julie. She felt like she was watching herself in a movie. It was all too perfect.

Throughout the entire evening, they snuggled under the blanket. Alex would kiss Julie with long, sensual kisses. The kind that stirred her down to her bones. During intermission, a young lady came in and handed Alex an envelope. When they opened it, they saw it was their picture. Alex put the photo back into the envelope and stuck it in his inside jacket pocket.

The concert lasted for nearly two hours. When "Can't Smile Without You," was played, they both sang along. Julie was having the time of her life. Later in the evening, when the song "Mandy" was played, Alex turned to Julie and told her he loved the name Mandy, and if he were ever to have a daughter, that would be her name.

As the evening progressed, it did start to sprinkle, an annoying little drizzle that was enough to give you bad hair and make you angry that it was ruining a perfectly wonder-ful night. Barry came out for the second encore. Right at the very end, the sky opened up. There was a deluge. People were scrambling for their cars. Alex took Julie by the hand and they ran toward the VIP parking area where they had left the car. But they got soaked. He kissed her in the rain outside the car and it didn't matter that they were being rained on. They didn't seem to notice.

Once inside the car, Alex turned on the heater. "I'm sorry you're so wet. I think we should go stay at my house for the night. I don't really want to drive back to Coronado this late in this kind of weather. Better I get you dry so you don't get sick...

Bernie needs you healthy for the trial on Monday." Julie just nodded her head yes.

Once down the hill, Alex made his way to Brentwood. He could hardly see from so much water. The freeway traffic was going slow. Alex turned off the music in the car so he could hear in case a problem arose while they were driving. It was pretty tense for the thirty minutes it took to get there.

When they arrived, the garage door opener didn't work and he had to leave the car in the driveway. The power was out all over the neighborhood. "Looks like we're going to have to make a run for it. Are you ready?"

"Sure. Let's do it. We're already soaked. What's a little more water?" They both made a run for the front door. The rain was relentless.

When they got to the front door, Alex turned the key and got them in and closed the door behind him.

"Stay here, I'll get you some towels. Why don't you get those wet shoes off?" He made his way into the house, leaving Julie in the entryway. He returned right away and handed her a big towel to wrap around herself, and used a smaller one to begin drying her hair. He kissed her several times while he dried her.

"I have some candles in the kitchen. Follow me."

When Alex lit the candles he had on a shelf above the sink, she could see a little of the house. It wasn't huge, but it looked spacious. It was all newly remodeled. All of the furniture looked new and a bit on the manly side. Definitely no flowered wallpaper in this place. She followed him into the den, where he took a remote control and turned on the fireplace.

"I thought the power was out?" she asked with a puzzled look on her face.

"This runs off batteries, and the fuel is propane. Pretty slick, huh?"

"Well, I'm certainly impressed."

"I'm going to show you to my room. You can get out of your clothes in there. I'll find you something dry to put on, and I'll change too. Grab a couple of those candles."

Julie did as she'd been told, and followed Alex upstairs. His room was very nice. It had a king-size bed and she could see an on suite. Alex walked into the closet and grabbed a ter-rycloth bathrobe for Julie and some sweatpants and a T-shirt for himself.

"Why don't you take this into the bathroom? I'll go down the hall and change. I'll meet you by the fire."

She stepped into the nice big bathroom. It had a sunken tub that looked like you could fit four people in. She peeled off her very wet new clothes, and even had to take off her new panties and bra. Everything was too wet to leave on. She found a brush on the counter and ran it through her hair. When she finished, she slowly walked down the stairs. She could see the light of the fire flickering. Alex was standing right next to it trying to dry himself off. It was cold in the room. That looked like a good place to be, so she walked up and stood right next to him.

"Can I get you anything?" he asked. "I have some wine or something else a little stronger to warm you?"

"No, I think I'm done for the night. I'm still full from dinner and I've probably had too much champagne as it is."

"Come here, let's sit on the couch for a bit until you get warmed up."

When they sat on the big leather couch, Alex grabbed a crochet blanket he had on the end and wrapped it around both of them.

"My mom made me this. She crochets all the time. She can make just about anything."

Julie snuggled up against Alex and put her head on his shoulder. She felt so intense around him. It never let up. The strong feeling of attraction was consistent the entire time he was around.

"I want to thank you for the most amazing evening of my life. I can't think of any other day I've had, that has been so perfect. Even the rain. It's amazing. Can you hear it? I think it's holding us prisoner so we don't have to leave."

"You may be right. But I'm okay with that. I don't want to leave. I could stay here with you in my arms forever. You are so terrific. I think I'm falling in love with you, Julie. I didn't look for this to happen. But I feel whole when I'm with you."

"Me too, Alex. I know I'm falling in love with you, too. What a mess, huh? Where were you four years ago, or two years ago? We have to make it work out. I know I want to be with you. Only you."

Alex began to kiss Julie. This time, it felt different. It was much more intense. He slid her back onto the couch and untied her bathrobe. He opened it slightly so he could get his hand inside. He felt her soft breast and ran his fingers around her nipple. It reacted quickly, hardening to his touch. Julie was in heaven. He was kissing her neck softly and touching her with such tenderness. The rain continued to pound on the roof, and the fire was the only light in the room. She sighed softly at his touch.

Alex ran his kisses down her neck toward her chest. He reached inside of the robe, now opening it to expose her beautiful, soft suppleness. He used his lips and tongue to kiss them tenderly. He was hard, and she was a hot mess. Her body reacted to him so quickly, it never took long for her to feel as if she could take him at any time. With his tongue, he continued to make his way lower, still massaging her breasts, until he reached her spot. Spreading her legs slightly, he kissed her and teased her with his mouth patiently until she exploded. He could hear her delight as she arched her back, inviting him in. Julie was in heaven. Never had she imagined making love could feel like this.

Once he knew she had been satisfied, he stood and removed his clothes, exposing himself to her in the firelight. She sat up and looked at him. He was beautiful. His body was perfection. His chest was chiseled, and short soft blonde curls trickled across it. His manhood was pleasing and she was delighted at the sight of his girth. Julie reached for his thighs and pulled him close to her. She'd never been in this position with a man before, but she knew she wanted to please him. Giving it her best shot, she took him between her hands and began gently teasing by rolling them around between her hands. Alex seemed to like it. He responded with a sound of pleasure she'd never heard come out of a man before. She then let him enter her mouth and he liked that even more. He had to stop her. It was too intense and he was afraid it would end too quickly.

Alex picked Julie up off the couch and sat down. He placed her on top of him. She wrapped her legs around his back. The anticipation was more than she could bear. She reached between them and found him, inviting him inside of her. As he entered her, they simultaneously made sounds of pleasure. She found him to be way more than she could have hoped for. Alex found himself inside a tight, hot oven moistened to perfection.

Julie kissed Alex strongly and longingly. She couldn't get close enough to him. He rocked her on his lap and she responded by pushing herself down harder. She wanted him deeper. As deep as she could get him. Letting go of her inhibitions for the first time of her life felt fantastic. She could be herself with him. She could react as she needed to because he wanted the same thing and she knew he wouldn't judge her. Alex sat back on the couch and continued to rock Julie with his hands on her hips. They were both almost animal-like in their reaction to one another. They enjoyed each other for as long as they could without giving in to their final urges. She wanted this to last as long as it could. But when they could no longer resist, Julie screamed with pleasure as they both exploded simultaneously into each other's arms.

Julie began to cry. It had been the first time she'd ever experienced an orgasm. It was an amazing feeling. She was sad that she hadn't had this in her life until now. All those years wasted.

"Are you all right? Why are you crying? Did I hurt you?"

"No Alex, I'm just sad I've never had this. I'm so glad it was with you. You are amazing. I don't ever want to leave your arms."

"Well, you were pretty amazing yourself. I'm going to have to tell Ms. Parker what a nasty girl you are." They both burst out with laughter.

Lying back down on the couch again, they fell asleep. Legs wrapped around each other and holding one another tight under the blanket. Listening to the sound of the rain and the fire. Julie had been satisfied for the first time ever. She loved this man. She knew she loved him and wanted to stay with him always.

Chapter 14

*J*ulie was suddenly aroused by the smell of coffee. When she opened her eyes, it took a minute to get her bearings. As soon as she realized where she was, she remembered last night. A big smile came over her face.

"Good morning, Sunshine. How's my girl this morning?"

Alex was walking into the room with two steaming mugs filled with the most intoxicating aroma. "I don't have doughnut holes, but I brought in the chocolate chip cookies we got from The Ivy last night. Sorry, I haven't been here so there's no food. It's the best I could do in a pinch."

Julie sat up and put the robe on. It was still cold, and she was suddenly feeling a bit self-conscious about being naked in the room with Alex. He handed her mug and sat next to her on the couch. Alex kissed her still exposed shoulder and she turned her face to meet his and get a kiss.

"You taste like chocolate chip cookies," she said laughing and taking a sip. "And this coffee is great. Did you save me a cookie?"

"Here," he said reaching into his pocket and producing a huge, delicious-looking cookie. Julie broke it in half and dunked it in her mug.

"You really are a dunker, aren't you? What time do you want to head back? I've got our clothes in the dryer. It shouldn't be too long. I thought you might want to go upstairs and take a shower."

"I'd love that. Can I use the bathroom in your bedroom?"

"Sure. You can do anything you want. Why don't you head on up and I'll bring the clothes when they are done."

Julie stood and gave Alex a kiss on top of his head. "I'm still trying to pinch myself about last night. The whole day and night, really. You are an amazing lover."

Alex stood and put his arms around Julie. He looked into her eyes and said to her.

"I love you, Julie Turner. You are terrific in every single way. I've never been so satisfied by a woman ever. Where did you learn to do that?" He was grinning from ear to ear.

"Actually, truth be told, I've never done anything like that before. But I'm a good listener. My best friend TJ and her husband Jack Danger have been going at it since high school. I've unfortunately walked in on them a few times. And she's been very descriptive about their love lives as long as I've known her. She was my college roommate. She used to go on about how they tried this and that. It was always very annoying. But now I'm glad I listened."

"Well, remind me to thank her when I meet her. And nobody's name is Jack Danger. Are you serious?"

"Serious as a heart attack. He is the 'Tire King' of the Carolinas. He has a commercial on TV and he says, 'If you need new tires, don't be a stranger. Come see Jack Danger!'

Corny but effective. He does very well," she said as she started upstairs. "See you up there!"

Alex watched as she made her way up. She had a great body, a tiny waist and great backside. He was starting to get hard again just watching her. After collecting the clothes out of the dryer, he ran up and placed them on the bed. He stood in the doorway to the bathroom and watched Julie as she slathered soap all over herself. He decided to surprise her and joined her.

"Oh, I've never taken a shower with anyone before. This is another first to check off my list."

"Well then, let me give you something else to check off your list." Alex picked Julie up and she kissed him as she wrapped her legs around him. He walked her over to the glass wall and pressed her up against it. He was easily able to find his way inside. She was amazingly welcoming and had no trouble sliding him in. He could barely control himself with her. He plunged into her with hard thrusts while she kissed him all over his neck and face. He was so aroused he couldn't control himself inside her. Her hands grabbed handfuls of his hair. She was reacting to him as if she was experiencing an out-of-body moment. It was such ecstasy she couldn't think straight. Once again, they exploded with each other and were so out of breath, Alex had to sit them both on the bench in the shower seat while they recovered.

"I think you're trying to kill me," he said laughing and kissing her lightly all over her face and neck. Alex washed Julie's hair and she loved it. She'd never had her hair washed before. He ran his fingers through it very sensually. She felt magnificent.

When they were dressed and ready to go back to Coronado, the rain was still coming down. But now it was light rain, and they drove in and out of it. Both of them were beaming. Julie was so happy. He had never seen her smile quite like that before. She was even more beautiful today than she'd ever been. And Julie had a feeling inside of having conquered. As if she had arrived. Like she was ready to take on the world and they'd better get out of her way.

"Do you want to come in?" she asked Alex while standing at her front door.

"I don't think I should. I know you need to get some rest tonight, and I have a lot of catching up on my work, too. This book is turning out to be more time-consuming than I thought. If I come in, we'll be up all night and neither of us will be worth a damn in the morning. I'll see you in court in the morning okay?" She reached for his neck and drew him into her. She kissed him good night and walked inside.

"Oh God, I'd better call TJ or she'll kill me!"

Chapter 15

*J*ulie was up early that morning. She was exhausted when she finally got off the phone with TJ, as she demanded to hear all of the details, and was thrilled for her friend. She'd slept better than she had her entire life. She felt as if she was ready for anything. The trial was starting and she'd prepared everything for the defense team in such a way, that everything that was needed would be at the court room and ready. Organization was one of her best traits. She knew where everything was. Every file, every piece of evidence, every piece of information about any and all witnesses was at the touch of her fingers.

She was dressed and out the door early and decided to drive straight to the courthouse. She wanted to get there early and try to avoid the news reporters and cameras. Driving her car to one of the rear doors of the courthouse, she asked for help in carting in the cases she had stored all of their paperwork. One of the guards was kind enough to assist her. Once inside, she paced and waited for everyone to arrive.

Not long after, she could hear the noise outside get very loud. Sure enough, Bernie and his co-chair were being attacked by the reporters. He loved all the attention as he walked into the courtroom, strutting like a peacock. After all, this is why he had taken this case pro bono. He needed the cameras to record as much fuss as he could for the good of the case and of course, his book. Alex arrived with Bernie and sat two rows behind them.

When their client entered the courtroom, Julie was blinded by the flashes of the cameras. It wasn't until the judge entered and ordered them to stop, that she was able to regain focus.

Their client sat in the courtroom with a smirk on her face the entire time. She kept fussing with her hair and looking at her fingernails. She was completely undisturbed by what was happening. She was more concerned at looking at the reporters and the TV cameras than the witnesses that were being called.

After the first day ended about three o'clock, everyone returned to the office. Bernie was beaming with excitement at all of the publicity. Ms. Parker had put a pile of messages on his desk from journalists all over the country who were requesting interviews. Alex was in Bernie's office the rest of the afternoon, taking notes of what was happening. Every once in a while, he would sneak a look out the glass at Julie, who struggled not to smile and tried to keep a straight face while she continued to work. She had to finish organizing the files for the next day's proceedings.

After five, most everyone had cleared out. Bernie left as well, on his way to meet friends at the Hotel Del for dinner and cocktails. He invited Alex, who bowed out with the excuse of work on the book.

"Well, Sunshine, your place or mine?" he asked with a wink. "I don't think I can go another minute without holding you in my arms."

"I have to go home first. I need to shower and get something to eat. I haven't had a bite all day."

"Well, go home and shower, but I'll take care of feeding you. Just bring your clothes over and you can stay with me tonight. We can leave from there tomorrow."

"Sounds great. More spaghetti?"

"I'll surprise you. Just hurry."

Alex walked Julie to her car. He didn't want to risk anyone seeing them being affectionate with each other in public, so he just closed her car door and went on his way toward his vehicle. Julie couldn't wait to be with him. She ran in the front door, throwing her clothes all over the floor and running into the shower. She packed a small bag with the things she would need in the morning and threw on another of TJ's pretty bra and panties. Pink ones this time. And just a pair of clean jeans and tank top.

When she pulled up in the circular driveway where Alex's guest house was, she could hear the sound of soft music playing from behind the gate. When she got to the door, it was open. Alex was in the kitchen. He had already opened a bottle of pinot and was whipping up something that smelled delicious.

"Come on in, Sunshine. Pour yourself a glass and watch the master at work."

"You are going to make someone a great little husband someday," she said as she poured wine into the two wine glasses and took a seat on the stool at the kitchen counter. Alex had showered and stood there in a pair of sweat pants and a T-shirt. His hair was wet, and he smelled of that cologne he always wore. She just watched as he prepared dinner for them. He looked so good to her. She was beside herself with joy.

Alex walked past her with two hot plates and set them on the table. He then walked up to where Julie sat on the stool, and stood right up against her. He put his arms around her, bringing her toward him. He began to kiss her and as he was standing so close, she could feel him harden as he held her.

"I couldn't keep my eyes off of you in court today. You were terrific! You are so hot when you are in the courtroom. If everyone could see what you hide inside that suit, the case would have been closed today! Come on, sit before it gets cold."

As they sat down to eat at the table, Alex lit a candle and brought the wine from the kitchen counter.

"How could you have done all of this so fast? Salad, chicken, green beans ... you are amazing!"

"Hardly. When you are a bachelor, you learn little tricks on how to feed yourself if you want to keep from starving. This was salad in a bag. I just cut up an avocado and threw some dressing on it. The chicken I got at the grocery store on the way home. I just cut it up. And the green beans were frozen. I just boiled them and there you have it."

"So, how are things going with the book?"

"Pretty good. I have an outline that Bernie likes now. So it's just a matter of plugging in the information as things progress, and getting him to approve it. I'm trying to keep up as I go along. But I've had some distractions, you know?" They both laughed and enjoyed the meal. When they were finished, Alex threw everything in the sink.

"Let's take a walk down to the beach. We'll walk off our dinner. It's a nice night and I could use the fresh air."

Alex took Julie's hand as they walked toward the beach. When they reached the sand, he kicked off his shoes and helped Julie take off her sandals. They walked toward the water. It was another star-filled night. Just chilly enough so he could put his arm around her as they walked along the shore. Alex kissed Julie as they walked and she was enjoying being in his arms. He made her feel so secure and so relaxed. They talked about the concert and were glad there was no rain to spoil their evening.

As they returned to his cottage, Alex closed the door and slipped off his T-shirt. He walked over to Julie, put his arms around her, and began to kiss her. His soft tongue circled the inside of her lips. He slipped his hands under her blouse and slipped it over her head. Julie began to feel herself reacting to his touch. He was always so tender. Not much was said, it was all understood. They knew what the other was thinking without words. Alex unhooked Julie's bra and slipped it off. He continued to kiss her as he softly squeezed her breasts. He picked Julie up and carried her into his bedroom, placed her on his bed and slipped off his pants. She loved the way he looked.

Always ready for her. He slipped off her jeans and panties and laid himself on top of her. He felt so right.

Now Julie was so hot she could hardly wait. He teased her breasts with his tongue and moved her spot with his wet finger, making her back arch and sigh with delight. He was a master at foreplay. She'd never had that. He held off until he knew they were both ready and then he let her welcome him in. He moved on her just right, and continued to kiss her neck, running his tongue up and down the side. Julie bent her knees up and opened herself more to, letting the penetration deepen. They both enjoyed the rocking and the jolting until they couldn't wait any longer. Julie begged him to finish her. Alex was more than happy to oblige. He eagerly lost control and exploded passionately as they both shouted blissfully.

Filled with satisfaction, they lay in each other's arms. Julie thought she was the luckiest woman alive to have found this man. A man that was perfect for her. They made love all night, without a care in the world. At that moment in time, they were the only two people alive. They thought of nothing else but enjoying each other. But soon enough, the stars turned into dawn, and the reality of the world crept into their special moment. They would have to go back to reality and to their work day until the next time they could steal away together.

The case continued for many weeks. Julie and Alex spent every night together in passion. They worked by day in a professional atmosphere. But at night and on weekends, they were inseparable.

They would go to the movies, take moonlight swims in the ocean, and picnic in the park under Julie's favorite tree. All the while, they maintained their privacy from the eyes of the work environment. They had fallen in love. A deep romantic love. And they planned a future with one another.

When the defense finally rested, they knew it was just a matter of time before the jury came back with a verdict. They were out only two days deliberating before coming back. The school teacher was found guilty on all counts. The judge wasted no time sentencing her to sixty-five years in federal prison with no possibility of parole. There would be no appeal. It would be useless, and Bernie had accomplished what he had set out to do. He'd had his day in the spotlight. Now it was just a matter of cashing in on the publicity and the book.

Chapter 16

One week after the trial, Alex had to return to L.A. for business. He would work on the book there for a couple of days before returning to Coronado to finish. He had to spend some much needed time with his father whose health was failing. Julie was busy at work, but was lost at home in the evenings. He would call and they would share their days on the phone for hours. But it wasn't the same. She missed him terribly and couldn't wait for him to return.

As Julie was at work one afternoon, two Marines walked into the office. Ms. Parker directed them to Julie, who was upstairs in the conference room. When Julie saw them walking up the stairs, she got a lump in her throat and felt weak in the knees. She dropped into a chair and felt like she couldn't breathe. They just stood in the doorway looking at her.

"We are looking for Mrs. Julie Turner," one of them said.

"I'm Julie Turner. Is it Brian? Is he dead?"

"Mrs. Turner, we are here to inform you that your husband has been injured in the line of duty. His company was ambushed and the vehicle he was traveling in was hit. He's alive, but has suffered some wounds and head trauma. Right now, he's on a medical Navy ship in the Gulf, but will be transferred here to Balboa Naval Hospital in a few days once he's stable. The Navy will contact you when he is state-side. You can see him then."

"Who can I speak to if I need more information?"

"Ma'am, that's all the information we have to give you at this time. I'm sorry."

The Marines turned and walked out just as quietly as they had arrived. Julie sat in the conference room in shock. One of the legal clerks saw them leave and asked if there was something she could do for her. She couldn't even respond. She just sat there. So many things were going through her head at that moment. She'd been so happy and involved in her bliss that the thought of Brian being overseas had only entered her mind when she was rehearsing how she would ask him for a divorce. But now, he was hurt. She couldn't just spring that on him when he was in a hospital bed. *What can I say to Alex? How will we deal with this?*

Bernie and Ms. Parker ran up the stairs to check on her. Bernie offered to drive her home, but she declined. He told her to go home and take some time off to do whatever she needed to do.

Julie drove home and called her mom. Then she called Mrs. Turner to see if she'd been notified as well. The Marines had just left their home and had given them no more information than she had gotten.

Julie called TJ to tell her what had happened. She couldn't believe it either. This had come out of left field and blindsided everyone. She told Julie to just hang in there and take it one day at a time until Brian was back. And then again, one day at a time. But time took too long to pass. She'd always wanted things done in the now. But it was all out of her control.

Later that night when Alex called, she told him what had happened that afternoon in the office, and that Brian was going to be flown to San Diego in a couple of days.

"Take all the time you need, Sunshine. You can't go asking for a divorce when a man is in a hospital bed. I'll understand. Just do what you feel you need to do. I'll be home tomorrow. I'll be there if you need me, any time you need me."

But Julie needed him now. She wanted him to come and just hold her and tell her everything would work out and they would be together. But something in the pit of her stomach was telling her it wouldn't be okay. And that she'd end up in a dead-end marriage for the rest of her life.

When Alex came back the next day, Julie wasn't home. He knew where she'd be. Under the tree in the park clearing her head, trying to figure out what to do. So he drove there, and he was right. She was sitting at the table with her head down between her arms. As he walked over to her, he could hear her sobbing. He felt terrible for her. They both knew the day would come when she'd have to confront her husband. But they surely didn't think it would be a day like this.

"Sunshine, I'm back." Julie threw her arms around Alex's neck and began to sob on his shoulder. He just held her and let her cry it out. He knew that is what she needed to do. After a short time, he told her to get in his car, and they drove to the cottage. He made her sit on the couch and fixed her some hot tea. He put his arm around her and kissed her tenderly, reassuring her of his love.

"I love you, Sunshine. I'll always love you. Things will work themselves out, you'll see."

"What if they don't? What if he comes back and he's too sick to deal with the divorce? What then?"

"You're putting the cart before the horse. Let's just see how things play out. All I know is that somehow, you and I will end up together. Have a little faith."

Alex and Julie sat on the couch most of the evening until she began to fall asleep. He carried her to the bed and held her through the night. She felt better now that he was back. He'd given her the strength to deal with whatever she had ahead.

In the morning, when she returned to her place and get dressed for work. She decided she needed to go to the office and immerse herself in work to get her mind off of everything. Alex had arrived to the office ahead of her. They didn't need to give anyone a reason for any suspicion regarding the two of them. Especially now. When Julie got to the office, no one said anything to her about what was going on. But she knew they were talking about it behind her back. No one there really even knew she was married. She'd always kept her private life out of the work place. Not even any photos on her desk. She was there to work and that was that. Now her private business was the *gossip du jour*. Good thing no one knew of her affair with Alex. That's the last thing they needed.

When she walked to her desk, there was the usual little white bag. Alex was so sweet. He'd brought her doughnut holes just as he always did. She could see him inside of Bernie's office going over the notes for the book. Bernie had agreed to be interviewed by a famous television news woman. They were setting up at the house for the taping in the early afternoon. Alex was going to go along so he could take notes and pictures. They were getting ready to leave, when Bernie came out of his office and called Julie in.

"Julie dear, is there any news of your husband? Is there anything Sylvia and I can do to help?"

"No sir, I'm afraid not. They say he'll be at Balboa Naval Hospital by the end of the week. I'll know more then. Thank you for your concern, though."

Julie walked back to her desk, and a few minutes later, Bernie and Alex walked past her on their way out. Alex tapped her desk lightly as he walked by. It was hard for her to concentrate. She was trying to wrap up the files from the school teacher's case they had just finished and had left a mess in the upstairs conference room. Her telephone rang just as she was getting ready to go up and finish her work. It was a nurse from the hospital letting her know that Brian would be there late that afternoon. Another blow. She wasn't expecting him quite so soon.

She would have to face him today. What would she say? Julie tried not to think about it. Her stomach was full of knots. Her hands were unsteady and she felt faint. Instead, she decided to bury herself in her work. She ran upstairs and tore into the files with a fury. She was determined to get it all in order that day so they could be placed in storage. By four o'clock, she was finished. Again the phone on her desk rang. It was the same nurse telling her that Brian had indeed arrived, and telling her where she could find him. Julie called Mrs. Turner to let her know in case they wanted to see him as well.

Julie wrote Alex a note and placed it in an envelope on his desk. She wanted him to know she was going to go to the hospital, and left.

As she crossed the bridge, she tried to practice what to say to him. Then she decided not to plan her speech because she didn't know what shape he'd be in. When she arrived on the medical floor, she checked at the nurse's station. The nurse took her into a small waiting room and told her one of the doctors would be in to talk with her. She waited for a few minutes before an older gentleman in a white coat walked in and introduced himself.

"Mrs. Turner, I'm Doctor Ramsey. I'll be taking care of your husband while he's recovering. I just wanted to brief you on his condition. Your husband was inside a military transport vehicle when a roadside bomb exploded. He's suffering from head trauma and severe hearing loss. He's in a lot of pain and we have him heavily sedated. Imagine being inside of a barrel and having someone turn on a jet engine in there. That's the intensity of the blast that's affected his hearing. He has loss of balance as well. He was also the only survivor. Everyone else perished. He's lucky to be alive. We expect him to fully recover, but it will take some time. You'll have to be patient with him."

Patient! Thought Julie. *I don't want to be patient. I want to end my marriage and move on with my life.* This was all happening too fast. She had gone from being perfectly happy and being in bliss, back to the stalemate of a marriage she no longer wanted. And once again, she wasn't in control of her life. But she knew she owed him this. After all, she'd been unfaithful to him while he'd been away.

"Please follow me. I'll take you to him." The doctor led Julie down the corridor past several rooms with double glass doors. He stopped in front of one that was dark. He told Julie to go inside and speak softly to him and hold his hand. That he would know she was there but probably wouldn't be able to respond.

At first, Julie couldn't move. Her feet were frozen to the ground. She just stood there and looked at him. Brian's head was wrapped in gauze bandages that held in place thick layers of some kind of dressing over his ears. She saw him turn his head in the direction of the door, and she realized he was awake. He lifted his right hand slightly, letting her know she should come close.

Julie stepped into the room and walked over to Brian's bedside. He looked at her as she stood next to the bed looking at him. She whispered, "Hi." Brian turned his head away and went back to sleep. He was hooked up to all kinds of equipment. She could see his heart beating on a monitor, and there were bags of fluid going into his veins. She sat down on a chair not knowing what to do next, and his parents walked in. Mrs. Turner walked over, took Brian's hand and she began to sob.

"Julie, how is he?" she asked.

"They said he would make a full recovery. But that it will take time. I guess he has some kind of hearing loss right now and a lot of head pain. They are keeping him sedated. "

The Colonel just looked at the two of them. "He's tough. He's a Marine. He'll be fine." And he turned and left the room. Mrs. Turner sat in a chair next to Julie and continued to cry. Julie felt like the life was being sucked out of her and started to leave.

"Where are you going?"

"I can't stay. I need to go back to the office and wrap up a few things so I can take some time off when I take him home. He needs his rest right now. My being here might agitate him. I'll call you." She picked up her purse and walked quickly to the elevator. It couldn't come up fast enough for her. By the time she got downstairs, she was practically sprinting to the front door. She felt as if she was having a panic attack and began gasping for air. Once she got inside her car, she began to scream and banged on the steering wheel. This isn't the way she planned it. She wanted to be with Alex. This wasn't supposed to happen. She sat there and cried hard asking herself, *why was this happening? I just wanted out.*

Once over the bridge, she drove straight to Alex's cottage. He was waiting for her. She ran inside and straight into his arms. He held her and comforted her. She told him what the doctors had told her. And she described Brian's condition and how he looked.

"This is going to take a while. I don't want to have to take him home with me. I just want to tell him about us and be done with it."

"You can't do that. We'll have to be patient. Just hang in there. I'll be here for you." Alex had a way of calming Julie. He always made her feel secure and relaxed. He suggested they take a walk down to the water and get some fresh air. But instead, they decided to climb into the shower, and ended up making love. As the water showered down on them, they clung on to each other tightly, and afterward went to bed. Their passion was fierce that night. They had no inhibitions with one another, ever. But tonight, their love making seemed epic. Something felt different. And they both felt it. They needed to reassure each other of their bond and fell asleep holding one another, exhausted and satisfied

Chapter 17

After two weeks, Brian was well enough to be released and go home. He still was not fully recovered. But he was becoming too anxious to remain in the hospital. Julie dreaded it. It would be the end of her time alone with Alex.

Alex had decided he would go back to L.A. until Julie could get Brian well enough to tell him she wanted out of their marriage. They both hated the idea, but for now there was nothing else they could do. So, they spent their last night at the cottage knowing that they had to make that night last until they could be together again. In the morning, Alex packed up his car, and Julie drove to Balboa Hospital to pick Brian up. She had taken a week off from work to care for him. Bernie had told her she should take as long as she needed, but a week was all Julie thought she could take. She didn't want to be around Brian any more than she had to. A nurse wheeled Brian downstairs and helped Julie put him in her car. She made sure the radio was off. Loud sounds still bothered him and he wore very dark tinted glasses. He said nothing to her as they crossed the bridge. Once at the house, he wandered around as if he was in a strange place. Julie went into the kitchen to prepare food.

He'd just stand in the doorway and look at her almost as if she was a perfect stranger.

When it was time to eat, he sat at the table in the kitchen with her. Finally, he uttered, "It looks good."

"Do you want to talk about it?" asked Julie, "I mean, about what happened? The doctor said it would be good for you to verbalize everything and get it off your chest."

"No," he said firmly.

Julie didn't press him any further. She figured it wasn't a good idea to piss him off. She remembered his bad temper and didn't want to set it off. He asked for his pills, and Julie told him he wasn't due for any medication for another hour. He got up from the table and picked up the bottle, opened it, and took one anyway. When Brian left the kitchen, Julie looked at the bottle and saw that he had been prescribed Oxycodone, a very strong pain medication. Brian laid down on the couch and she cleaned up the kitchen. He still wasn't talking, so she decided she'd take a shower. When she finished, she heard Brian snoring on the couch and decided to leave him there. She had no desire to lay in a bed with him. She missed Alex so much it hurt.

During the night, she heard Brian talking loud in his sleep. He was having bad dreams and would shout out. She didn't move. She was afraid of what he would do if she tried to wake him up.

For days, he just walked around the house. He didn't want to shower or brush his teeth. He hardly ate. It was as if she wasn't even there with him. But he didn't miss a pill. She was afraid he'd get used to taking them and that worried her. They were very addictive. Once in a while, she would catch him talking to himself as if he was giving a speech.

That next Friday, Julie drove him back to Balboa Hospital to meet with Dr. Ramsey. When they took Brian to have an MRI, Dr. Ramsey took the opportunity to have some time with Julie.

Julie told him of his odd behavior. She expressed her concern about the pills.

"I think his recovery is going to take a long time. We really don't think he'll ever be the same. He certainly won't ever be deployed for combat again. His injury isn't just physical. He's suffered a great emotional injury as well. I hope you're prepared for this. You'll be all right. You are a Marine Corps wife," said Dr. Ramsey in a very condescending manner.

Julie didn't want to hear that. She needed to get away somewhere to call Alex. She hadn't talked to him in a week, and it was making her crazy. When she got Brian home, it was late. She told him that she needed to go to the grocery store and she'd be a while. But instead, she drove to her office. It was five-thirty by the time she got there and everyone was gone. No one stayed late on a Friday. Making sure no one would see her if they drove by, she parked down the street. She ran upstairs to use the phone in the conference room and dialed his number.

"Oh my God, it's so good to hear your voice! I miss you so much! Brian is acting worse than before he left. He won't talk to me. He just walks around in a vegetative state and talks to himself. I'm going to go crazy if I don't see you soon," she said as she cried.

"You know we can't see each other now. As much as I want to hold you in my arms, you need to hang in there until the doctors can get him better."

"The doctor told me today he'd never be the same. I can't stay with him forever. What about us?"

Alex paused for a few moments. "Julie, I can't take another man's wife when he needs her the most. It just isn't right. Let's see what happens in another couple of weeks. We'll decide what to do then. I love you. Don't forget that. I'd give anything to be with you but right now, he needs you."

Julie began to cry even harder. She didn't want to hang up the phone. It was the only lifeline she had to Alex. She knew the minute she put that phone down, she'd have to go back to missing him again.

"I love you, too. I'll call you again when I can. I'll be going back to work Monday. We'll figure something out."

When they hung up, Julie decided to call TJ. She hadn't had a chance to call her since she took Brian home. Julie was afraid to be on the phone in the house. She knew he would be listening to her every word.

"Hey girlfriend," said the friendly voice at the other end of the phone. "How are you holding up?"

"Not good. Brian isn't speaking to me. He's acting all crazy." Julie began to tell TJ what the doctor had told her, and about Brian's pill popping. She couldn't stop crying. She'd been holding all her emotions in all week and needed to let them all out. TJ listened to her dear friend. She knew Julie was in pain and wished she could be there to console her.

"I wish I could be there to help you. I don't know what to tell you to do. But if the doctors said he's not going to recover, do you have the heart to tell him you don't want to be his wife anymore? Do you think you can break his heart and walk away with another man when he needs you the most? I don't know what I'd do if I were you. I've never heard you so happy and I know you deserve that. But you took a vow "in sickness and in health." Only you can make a decision you'll be able to live with, darlin'. It's a tough one, but this has to be your call. Why don't you give it another week before you go all crazy about it? See how things go for a little while. He may get better. You never know? Alex will still be there. He told you so. Call me when you can all right?"

Julie knew TJ was right. She should give it a little while longer. It was too soon to see how Brian would do. She always felt better after she spoke with her. TJ was her rock. She found a tissue and blew her nose. As she picked up her purse, she suddenly felt the need to throw up. She ran down to the ladies room and dry heaved. *This is really getting to me. I need to pull myself together. I'd better eat something. It'll make me feel better,* she said to herself, realizing she hadn't eaten all day.

Julie washed her face and combed her hair. Brian would wonder what took her so long, so she made a quick trip to the grocery store and ran home to fix dinner. Once again, he didn't eat much. He barely uttered two words to her. But while they were at the dinner table, he caught Julie by surprise. He reached across the table and squeezed one of her breasts. Then he got up and walked out of the kitchen.

She didn't know how to react. That had come out of the blue. Grateful that he hadn't initiated anything else, she cleared the table and went into the bathroom and locked the door. She stepped into the shower and began to cry again, sticking a wash cloth in her mouth so he couldn't hear her sobbing. How she wanted this to be over, how she wanted time to hurry up and pass so she could move on with her life. She stood in there until the hot water ran out. When she was done, she threw on her robe and walked out of the bathroom. Brian was asleep on the couch again. The TV was on. So she crept into the bedroom and crawled into bed, hoping he would stay out there again. She kept listening to him shouting out in his sleep and pacing around. But he didn't come in to bother her.

That Sunday, her mom and Brian's mom came to visit Brian. They had called and said they were coming to visit. Julie tried to get Brian to shower and shave for them and he finally obliged.

When they arrived, Brian sat on the couch and watched TV while they tried to visit with him. He was as unreceptive to them as he'd been to Julie. Julie's mom caught her in the kitchen as she was making coffee for them. "Honey, I know this is hard for you. We know how much you love Brian. But that'll get you through this, you'll see. Love always takes charge of things."

Julie wished she had the nerve to tell her mom everything. She got teary-eyed. Her mom thought it was because of Brian's condition, but Julie wanted to spill it all out to her. She wished her mom could fix things and make it better for her like when she was a little girl. Mom always made things better. But this was not to be. How could she tell her mom how miserable Brian had made her? How could she tell her mom she had been having an affair with a man who made her truly happy and who was the love of her life. What would her in-laws think of her if they found out that she had cheated on their Marine Corps son while he was away fighting for their country?

Julie realized right then this wasn't going to go away. She knew she was going to be forced to stay in this love-less marriage and have to sacrifice her own happiness for a vow she'd taken. It was all making her sick to her stomach. It was too much for her.

In the morning, Julie got up and got dressed or work. Brian was standing at the front window just looking out.

"I'm leaving for work. I left you a sandwich in the fridge. Will you be all right?" she asked and got no reply. He just looked at her and went into the kitchen to get some coffee.

"Well then, call me at the office if you need anything. I'll try not to be too late." Julie walked out the door and got into her car as fast as she could. She couldn't get away from there any faster. She felt as if she'd been locked up in a cage for over a week. When she got to the office, everyone asked about Brian. Everyone except Ms. Parker. Julie really didn't want to hear anyone's concerns. But she managed to say he was coming along. She looked at the empty cubicle next to hers. It was all she could do not to cry. There was no Alex.

There was no little white bag of doughnut holes on her desk. She just took a deep breath and tried to figure out what she needed to get accomplished that day. As she began to make a list, her phone rang.

"Hi, Sunshine. Do you miss me?" A big smile came over Julie's face.

"I miss you so much. When can you come?"

"I'm tied up here in L.A. I have a job interview today with one of the studios. They're looking for a writer for a TV show, and I'm seeing someone about it this afternoon. And, I'm on a deadline with Bernie's publisher. So it probably won't be for another week or two before I can get down there. My dad isn't doing too well, either. I'm sorry. I wish I had better news. How are things at home?"

"Not good. He's not coming around. And he's taking pain pills like they are going out of style. I don't know what to do. I was just glad to be able to get away and come to work today. The less I have to stay there the better. Alex, it's not looking good. I'm so depressed. I wish you were here to hold me." Julie's eyes were beginning to tear up. She tried to control it. She didn't want anyone at work to see her like that.

Alex sighed on the other end of the phone. Julie could hear that he wasn't happy either. "Let's see how things go in a little while. By the time I can come down, maybe he'll have turned around. I gotta go, Sunshine. I love you."

"Me too. Talk with you soon. Good luck with the interview."

Now she'd heard his voice. Her day would get better.

But the day turned into another week. And Julie was going crazy inside having to deal with Brian at home. She lived for Alex's daily phone calls, a luxury they didn't have on the weekends.

One night after he'd been home for more than two weeks, Julie was asleep. She was startled awake with Brian climbing on top of her.

"What are you doing? She asked.

"What do you think I'm doing?" he responded. He pulled her nightgown up around her face. She struggled to get out from under him, but he was determined. He spread her legs apart and found his way inside of her. The smell of him sickened her. She hated that he was touching her.

"Didn't you miss this, baby?" he said as her grinded her. "Didn't you miss this?"

Julie didn't fight any more. She knew the more she lay still, the sooner it would be over with. As always, he finished without any consideration to her needs. To him, she was just his toy. Something he could use to pleasure himself with. When he was done, he rolled over on the bed. Julie was afraid to move, so she waited. He began to snore not too long afterwards. So she crept off the bed and went into the bathroom and locked the door. She got into the hot shower to wash him off of her. She hated that he'd invaded a part of her that she now considered Alex's. She placed the wash cloth in her mouth again and cried as she scrubbed herself clean. She cried and sat on the bathtub floor curled up into a ball, and let the hot water run over her. This she knew she wouldn't be able to live with. Not now that she knew what making love was. Not knowing that she could be loved by a man who put her first. She felt sickened by what had just happened and began to throw up again. Morning couldn't come quick enough for her. She wanted to be able to leave for work and get away from him.

She stayed on the couch until dawn. Then she left for work early. She had no intention of being there when he woke up. There was no way she was going to let him touch her again. She drove down to the park and sat under her tree. She thought of all the times she'd been there for a quick lunch with Alex, and the afternoons they had spent in the park having a picnic or just enjoying a lazy weekend afternoon. She could feel his presence there. She felt so lost without him.

Chapter 18

After another week, Brian began to leave for the base early in the morning. The doctor had told him not to drive, but he said his hearing was improving and he couldn't sit at home any more. He got cleared to drive only to the Naval Amphibious Base right there on Coronado. He was supposed to be gone only a few hours a day. But he never listened. He began to stay on base longer and longer. He said he was just at the Quarterdeck office helping out. But Julie wasn't convinced that was what he was doing. He continued taking more and more pills. And as long as he left her alone, she didn't really care.

Dr. Ramsey had told Julie and his parents that Brian should be treated with kid gloves for now, that his emotional health was fragile. Having lost most of his team was something he'd have to work through. But he refused to go to any counseling. Dr. Ramsey told Julie Brian didn't need any more pills. But he kept coming home with them. She didn't know where he was getting them. And he'd begun to drink more and more every day.

Brian's parents and hers were trying to be supportive. But the pressure was all on Julie. By now, she knew leaving him was out of the question. She had no choice but to stay with him and try to be the good little wife everyone expected her to be. And she would have to break the news to Alex. But she didn't want to do it over the phone. This was something she'd have to do in person when she saw him. And he was coming this weekend to bring a draft of the book to Bernie.

Julie and Alex arranged to meet at the park after Alex was done visiting with Bernie and Sylvia. They were going to see each other there and then decide where to go. Julie couldn't wait to see him and hold him. It seemed like an eternity since she'd kissed him.

When that Saturday morning came, Brian told Julie he was going to drive to his parents' house and asked if she wanted to ride along. She declined, telling him she was going to go to the office to catch up on work for a case she was doing. She hated lying to him, but it was a necessary lie.

After he left, she quick took a shower and looked for something to wear. She wanted to look nice for him. Her heart was breaking inside. She prayed the words would come. She left so she could be on time. She wanted to be there first.

At three o'clock, she was already waiting there when Alex pulled up. When she saw him, she ran to put her arms around him. He swung her around and kissed her.

"Oh, I've missed you so much. You look terrific!"

Julie didn't want to let him go. They held hands and walked over to the tree where she'd put down a blanket for them to sit and talk.

"You look great too. I missed you so much, Alex. My days are so long and I think about you all the time. I can't get enough of looking at you right now." Julie was examining his face. His emerald green eyes looked tired. His face looked troubled.

"How did Bernie like the book? When is the actual publishing date?" she asked to break the ice.

"Well, we're shooting for November. Just in time for Christmas. I don't know who would actually buy a book like that as a gift, but that's what he wants. And he's writing the checks. I got the job at the station. We start drafting for the show on Monday." Alex was searching Julie's face intently, searching for a clue of what she had to tell him. He didn't want to say goodbye to her. He wanted her in his life more than anything.

"That's wonderful news! I'm so proud of you. I'll be sure to tune in when it goes on the air."

Julie was making small talk. She was just making the time pass and avoiding the inevitable.

"Sunshine, what aren't you telling me? I know something is bothering you. It's written all over your face. Just tell me what's going on." Alex lifted Julie's face between his hands. He gave her a soft kiss on the forehead. He could smell her scent and took a deep breath.

"I can't leave him now, Alex. I just can't leave him. God, I wish I could, but there is so much pressure on me to stay with him. He isn't well. I don't know how things are going to turn out with him. But for now, I just can't tell him I want out. The doctor says he needs to heal emotionally as well as physically. He lost everyone on his team. He isn't wanting to talk about it, and he's trying to dull the pain with Oxycodone and alcohol.

I want to die, Alex. I just want to die!" She lowered her head. She didn't want him to see the pain in her face.

By now, Julie was crying so hard she could hardly speak. Alex held her close to him. They laid down on the blanket and he held her while she let it all out. He was quiet. His eyes were filled with tears and could hardly focus on the leaves on the tree above him.

"I had a feeling this was going to happen and I was afraid I'd get my heart broken," he said as the tears ran down his face and mixed with hers. "But I wouldn't have given up this time with you for anything in the world. You are my Sunshine. And you'll always be in my heart. We need to be strong and make a clean cut. No more phone calls. No more seeing one another. You need to concentrate on your marriage if you're going to make it work. And I can't take it. Loving you and not being able to be with you will tear me apart. I know it's hard, but we have to do it."

Julie sat up and ran her hands through his blonde hair. She wiped his tears and kissed his cheek. Alex sat up and looked at Julie. He was trying to memorize every little thing about her. "You have to promise to call me if things go bad and you can leave him. You know I'll always be there for you. But I won't interfere unless you come for me and tell me it's okay. I want you to be happy. And you have to promise me something. You have to promise me that if you are not involved with anyone, and you still remember me, you'll come here twenty years from today. We'll come and see each other and reminisce about our love affair. Not too many people can say they found their perfect love. Even if it was only for a little while. I'll always remember this as one of the best days of my life. So, we'll come see each other here, just like in that Cary Grant movie. Is that a date?" Alex wiped Julie's face. He forced a smile and tried to make things easier for her. But his heart was breaking inside.

"What if I'm fat and ugly?" she said, half laughing.

"What if I'm bald and fat? Would you run away when you saw me?" They both giggled.

Julie hugged Alex as he helped her to her feet. She whispered in his ear, "I know you're right about this. It's just that it hurts so badly. I feel like my heart is being ripped out of my chest."

"Wait for me. I'll be right back." She watched as Alex ran over to his trunk and came back with a box cutter. He walked over to the tree and carved 'A+J' and then he put a heart around it. "We'll see how much the tree has grown when we come back. I love you so much, Sunshine. Don't disappoint me. Be here, okay?"

Julie nodded and choking through the words, she managed to say "Okay."

Alex knew it was time to part. Staying any longer would just prolong the pain. He walked Julie to her car and held the door open for her. She turned and they held one another for a long time. She tried to control the sobbing. He kissed her and she got into the car. He stayed and looked at her through the window as she waved at him one last time, and drove away. She barely made it home. She couldn't see to drive through the tears in her eyes. Her heart was broken into a million pieces now and she felt as if the air had left her body. Dragging herself in the house, she called TJ to tell her what she'd just done. She wanted to talk with her before Brian got back.

"Well girlfriend, it's probably for the best right now. This takes the pressure off of you and maybe you can help Brian get better. My heart is broken for you. I wish I was there."

"I wish you were here too, TJ. I'd make you help me pack up and we'd run away. Like Thelma and Louise!" They both laughed. "I feel so sick. This whole thing is making me feel sick to my stomach. And I'm so tired all the time. I can't eat. I don't even care if I die. I just want to crawl up into a ball and wake up twenty years from now." Julie blew her nose. It was dripping onto the phone. Her tears wouldn't stop. She was a nervous wreck.

"Hmmm, when was the last time you had a checkup? You have to take care of yourself too, you know? You should make an appointment. Maybe the doc will give you some Valium or whatever they are using these days to help you cope for a while."

"You're right. I'll call tomorrow and make an appointment. I haven't had a checkup in a long time. And even those pills sound good right now. I could use some sleep. Thanks. I'll call you soon. Love you. Thanks for always being there for me."

"Oh, don't you worry about it. I'd expect you to be there for me if Jack Danger ever went all whack on me and we had to shoot him and burry the body!" They both got a good laugh before they hung up. Julie tore her clothes off and got under the covers. It was cold and she missed Alex holding her in bed and warming her. She didn't expect Brian to come home to eat and she didn't care. She didn't want him there any way. As she laid there in the darkness she wished she were like Rip Van Winkle, closing her eyes and wake up in the future so she could see Alex again. She closed her eyes and tried to picture his face in her mind. That smile he gave whenever he saw her. The way his soft blonde hair fell over his ears. The way his green eyes squinted when he laughed. She didn't want to forget. He had made her feel so loved in so many ways. In the back of her mind, she knew no one could ever live up to him. He had been her one true love. And she felt more trapped than ever in her marriage.

Rain began to hit the roof. It was as if the heavens were sad for them too. She began to cry again, remembering the first time they made love after they had gotten soaked at the concert. She fell asleep remembering that first time. Alex had really shown her what making love was really all about.

When Monday morning came, she wanted to call in sick and stay in bed all day. But she didn't want to risk being home if Brian was there. So she forced herself up and out the door. She didn't even shower. She just washed up and got dressed as quietly as she could. He had come home during the night and was passed out on the couch. He reeked of hard liquor. Pills were scattered on the coffee table where he must have dumped the bottle. She crept past him and drove directly to the office.

When she arrived, Ms. Parker had put some messages on her desk. Bernie had asked if she could take a client who was coming in that afternoon.

As she sat down, she tried not to look to the side where Alex had used the desk next to hers. Everyone was going about their business as if nothing had changed. And it hadn't. Not for anyone but her. Her life would never be the same again.

Julie decided to look at her rolodex and call her doctor for an appointment. She had promised TJ that she'd go and get checked out. She was emotionally drained and had been feeling like hell. When she dialed the doctor's office and the receptionist answered, she was informed that her last office visit had been two years before and was way overdue. She was lucky someone had just cancelled their appointment and managed to get a visit scheduled for the next morning. She was actually looking forward to going and getting something to help her calm her nerves and maybe sleep. Sleep was going to be her salvation. She wanted not to have to be conscious any more than she had to be. Being awake meant that she'd be constantly remembering how miserable she was without Alex. Sleep and work. That's all she wanted to do.

Chapter 19

*J*ulie watched as the nurse walked out of the exam room closing the door behind her. She stood there looking down at her hands. The gown she'd been given to put on was flimsy at best. As she disrobed, she folded her clothes neatly and placed them on a stool behind the curtain, and then tried to figure out how to stick her arms through the pink cloth contraption. It had ties in the back that didn't seem to match up. After trying a few times to tie it, she gave up and just took a seat at the end of the exam table. There was a sheet there and she placed on her lap. The table top was cold and stuck to the back of her thighs. As she waited, she looked around at the familiar room. Everything looked the same as it had when she had last visited. Same pale blue walls, same flower paintings on the walls. The room was dimly lit. She waited only a few minutes before Dr. Lowry walked through the door. She stopped briefly as if she were in shock and addressed Julie.

"My, my. Who do we have here? It's been a while hasn't it?" Dr. Lowry smiled and walked over to Julie and began to shake her hand. She was a striking red head in her mid-thirties with freckles, probably not very much older than Julie was. She always had a great smile and a sweet calmness about her.

"I don't believe I've seen you since you got married. How's that going?"

Julie didn't know quite how to respond, so she lied and politely said, "Just fine."

"So tell me, what seems to be the matter?"

Dr. Lowry took a seat on the stool across from Julie and began thumbing through the chart as Julie began to discuss her symptoms.

"I'm so tired all the time. I can't seem to eat. Nothing sounds good to me. In fact, I've even gotten queasy a couple of times. I know I've been working a lot, but I can't seem to eat anything. I've been way more tired than usual. I think it may be my nerves. My husband returned from his deployment with injures and I've had to deal with all of his problems. My nerves seem to be on edge. Really I was hoping to get something to help calm me down a little and maybe help me sleep more soundly."

Dr. Lowry looked at Julie with a concern. "I'm so sorry to hear about your husband, Julie. I hope he'll be all right soon. Well, let's take a look at you."

Dr. Lowry began to listen to Julie's Heart and lungs with her stethoscope. Julie just about jumped off the table when she placed it on her back. It was cold! Then, she felt the glands on Julie's neck and then she asked her to lie back. She began poking on her abdomen and under her rib cage.

"Does it hurt when I do this?" she asked as she pushed down under her ribs.

"No, not at all."

"Good. Now let me have you put your feet on the stirrups and slide down to the edge of the table. I'm going to take a pap smear while you are here. We should take a look at the IUD, too. It's been a while since I put it in."

Julie put her feet on the stirrups and slid down to the end of the table. Dr. Lowry placed a speculum and Julie could feel a slight scraping as she took the sample. She laid there looking forward to it all being over soon. She tried to focus on the picture on the wall. As she waiting for her to finish, she felt Dr. Lowry slightly tugging at something.

"I'm going to remove this IUD. It really needs to come out. You'll just feel a little pressure now. Try to relax. Take a deep breath and let it all out. There, all done," she said, and she stood up. She began the manual exam of Julie's uterus.

"When was your last period?"

"I don't remember. I've never been very regular, so I don't really keep track."

"Julie, I'd like to get a little blood while you're here. I'm going to send the nurse in to give you a little poke and then I'll be back in. Does that sound all right? You can sit up now but stay right where you are."

Julie just nodded her head. She didn't care what they did to her. She just wanted to get her prescription and get the hell out of there. She sat and waited until the nurse came in and drew a couple of vials of blood. As she waited on the end of the table, she began to get cold. It seemed like a long time before Dr. Lowry returned to the exam room. She took a seat on the stool again. She smiled at Julie.

"Well, I think we've figured out what part of your problem might be. You are pregnant, young lady. Congratulations!"

Julie's mouth dropped open. Dr. Lowry watched the color drain out of Julie's face. The news caught her by surprise and she couldn't speak.

"Julie, are you all right? I know this is sometimes a surprise but you look like you are in shock? I'm going to do a quick ultrasound so we can see how things are, okay? Lie back down for me."

Julie didn't know what to think but she did as she was told. She didn't want to be pregnant. She assumed the baby would be Brian's, and that's the last thing she wanted. That would trap her even further in their marriage.

Dr. Lowry rolled a small ultrasound machine over to the side of the exam table. She lowered down the sheet that was draping Julie to just below the navel. "Now I'm going to put some warm gel on your tummy. This won't hurt a bit."

Julie watched still in shock, as Dr. Lowry gently pushed a wand across her stomach, stopping to look for a minute in different places.

"There you are. Julie, look here. Do you see that small little thing moving there? That's your baby's heart beating. I'd say you are just about twelve weeks pregnant. Everything looks good, too."

"Twelve weeks? Did you say twelve weeks?" Right away, she began doing the math in her head. Twelve weeks ago, Brian still wasn't home. It wasn't his baby. It was Alex's baby! Now what was she to do? How would she tell Brian? How would she tell Alex, and how was she going to explain this all to her parents?

Dr. Lowry told Julie to step into the front office and schedule her next pre-natal care visit. She gave her a prescription for vitamins and left the room. Julie just sat there on the edge of the table. What had just happened? Now what was she going to do?

As she got into her car, she thought of everything she was going to have to do. There were too many things to sort through. She was going to go home and call TJ. She'd know what to do. She raced home and looked at the clock. She knew TJ would be at work, but she didn't care. Brian wasn't home, so she grabbed the phone, kicked off her shoes and began to dial the private line.

Pick up, pick up, pick up, she said to herself as she heard the phone ring. When TJ answered, she asked her if she could talk.

"Why, I always have time for you. What in the world is the matter? You sound simply crazy!"

"I went to the doctor for that exam."

"Well Darlin', are you dyin' or something? What in the world is wrong with you?"

"Dying? I wish I was dying! That would make everything easier. It's worse! I'm pregnant! I'm twelve weeks pregnant!"

"Geez girl, haven't you ever heard of Trojans? Where was your head?"

"I don't know. I had an IUD put in, but I guess it expired or something. It got old and I wasn't thinking about that. What should I do? What am I going to do?"

"Darlin', you just can't spring this on me and expect me to know what to do. I have to give this some thought now. You just calm your pretty little head down and don't say anything to anyone. We'll figure something out. Just try to calm down! You have to take care of yourself now. Especially now!"

"Okay. I won't say anything to anyone. I'll think about everything and you think of everything and we'll talk, okay?"

"That's my girl. Try to get some rest and we'll talk later. I love y'all. You know I do. Everything is going to be all right."

When Julie hung up the phone, she noticed the message machine was blinking. She put down the receiver and pushed play. It was Brian's doctor.

"Mrs. Turner, this is Dr. Ramsey. I just wanted you to know that your husband has missed his last three counseling appointments and the last three group support sessions. I have it on good authority that he's been on base at Camp Pendleton visiting the Enlisted Men's Club until closing time. I hope he has shared with you why he's been avoiding treatment, or perhaps he has just been under the weather. Either way, please ask him to re schedule. It's important. He needs help. He also shouldn't be mixing the pain medication he is taking with alcohol. I apologize if this is alarming to you, but we need your help getting him back into treatment. Thank you."

Great, she thought. *One more thing to worry about.* Julie knew Brian had been drinking and coming in late. But she'd been so miserable, she really hadn't wanted to deal with him. Nor had he been forthcoming about what he'd been doing or where he'd been. And she really hadn't wanted to give him the time of day. He'd been avoiding her just as much as she had been avoiding him. But now she'd been left with no option than to confront him. When was the question? He was never home when she was. He would come home during the night and sleep on the couch. He made the entire house smell like a distillery. The odor permeated the air in the entire house and it reeked as she got ready to go to work in the morning. But she wasn't about to ask him about anything. He wouldn't have spoken to her about it even if she'd tried. But right now, she just wanted to concentrate on the baby. What was she going to do? Should she tell Alex? As she sat there trying to figure out what to do first, she suddenly began to feel sick. She ran into the bathroom and barely made it to the toilet. When she finished, she rinsed her mouth out and decided she needed to lie down until the queasiness passed. She went into the bedroom and pulled the blanket over her head. She was out like a light in no time.

Julie was awakened by the sound of pounding on her door. She sat up and looked at the clock. It was three in the afternoon. *Have I been asleep that long?* The pounding was persistent, so she ran to the door to see who it was, still feeling groggy and not quite awake. When she opened the door, she was taken by surprise. There stood two Marines in uniform looking quite serious.

"Mrs. Turner? May we come in?"

"Of course. What's happened?" Julie opened the door and let the two men inside.

"Ma'am, we think you should sit down. We need to speak with you about an incident."

Julie did as she was asked to do. She was thinking it was about the missing appointments and didn't see what was coming.

"Mrs. Turner, we regret to inform you, that your husband was killed in a car accident early this morning. He was leaving base around two in the morning and was apparently going at a very high speed. From what the investigation shows, at the time of the accident, he was taking a curve way too fast and lost control of his vehicle. His truck overturned and slammed into a concrete barrier. He was pronounced dead at the scene of the accident. We're very sorry for your loss ma'am."

It took a few moments for the words to register. "You mean Brian is dead?"

"Yes ma'am. His remains are at the morgue on base. We need you to come with us as a formality. We need you to identify the body. We're very sorry."

"Do his parents know?"

"Yes ma'am. We have Marines at their home right now notifying them as well. Please, we need you come with us?"

"Sure, yes of course. I'll just grab my purse and comb my hair." Julie was still trying to grasp what they had just said to her. She was still in a kind of sleep stupor.

She ran a brush through her hair, grabbed her purse and walked out to meet the Marines. They led Julie into the back seat of a government vehicle. She sat quietly all the way to the base. Her mind was blank most of the time. But many things ran through her thoughts. Too many to make sense of all at once. Everything was piling up and she chose not to deal with any of her problems right at that moment. Trying to make her thoughts quiet, she just wanted to do what she needed to do, and beyond that, what would be next? She'd been miserable with Brian the last couple of years. But she certainly hadn't wished him dead. She'd just wanted him to get better so she could exit the marriage without guilt. Now, all she felt was guilt. Her husband was dead, and she was carrying another man's child. It was like living in the middle of a soap opera.

Once on base, she was taken to a small room at the medical building. Julie saw Brian's parents already waiting. As she entered the room, she could hear his mother crying. His dad was standing next to her. When they saw her, they both stood up and ran over to embrace her. They didn't say anything. They just stood there. Mrs. Turner continued to cry. Julie couldn't cry. She tried to figure out why. Maybe it was the shock. She felt bad and she knew she should be crying. But she just couldn't.

After a few minutes, a man in a lab coat came in and expressed his sympathies to all of them. He then led them down a hall to a room in the back. When they entered the room, they saw Brian laying on a stretcher with a white sheet pulled up to his neck. There was dry blood all over his hair and face. Brian's mom dropped to her knees and cried even harder. Julie just stood there staring at her dead husband, not being able to say a word. The man in the lab coat put his arm around her and led her back outside into the first room they had been in.

"Mrs. Turner, I know this is probably too much to ask right now, but we will need you to make arrangements for burial.

Or if you'd like, we can take care of that right here on base and you wouldn't have to worry about anything. We just need you to tell us where the remains are to be buried and we'll take care of that too."

"Yes please, make the arrangements. I wouldn't know what to do. I'll ask his parents, but I would imagine they will probably want him at the veterans' cemetery in San Diego."

"Can I have someone drive you home?"

"No. I'd like to go to my parents' house. Will you take me there?"

"Of course. I'm very sorry for your loss."

A few minutes later, the two men who had driven her to the base walked into the room and led Julie back outside to the car again. When they pulled into the driveway, Julie's parents ran out to meet her. The Turners had called them and they already knew. They put their arms around her and they went inside.

Chapter 20

After the service was finished, Julie walked over to Mrs. Turner and handed her the flag that had been used for Brian's casket. TJ got into the limo with Julie and the Turners. They drove back to their home. Once there, her father went upstairs. Julie, her mom, and TJ went into the kitchen. They sat on the chairs at the kitchen table. Her mom reached over and took Julie's hands.

"What are you going to do, sweetheart?" her mom asked. "Are you going to stay in your apartment?"

"Well, when TJ arrived, we had a chance to talk about a lot of things. I think I would like to make a fresh start some place new. I'm going to leave with her for Raleigh. I've never been out of California except when I went to her wedding and I liked it there. I just don't think staying here is in my best interest. Too many memories good and bad. I just think I need a fresh start. But there is something I need to tell you. I can't bring myself to tell daddy, so I'm going to have to rely on you to tell him later on. I'm just going to come out and say it. I had an affair. And I'm pregnant."

Julie's mom just sat there and stared at her daughter. Her mouth open as if she was waiting to hear more. But there was just an awkward silence. The three of them just sat there and looked at one another.

"Well, I don't know what to say dear. I knew you were unhappy in your marriage. But I had no idea. I'm not going to judge you in any way. I don't know what you were living with in your home. But I knew it wasn't good. But an affair....I take it the baby isn't Brian's?"

"No, mother. It's not."

"Are you going to tell the father?"

"I haven't decided yet. I haven't gotten there. I wanted to get through the funeral first and then make some decisions. I just don't know how I feel about that yet."

"Oh dear, what will the Turners think?"

"That's another reason I want to leave. I don't think it's going to be good for them to deal with all of this so soon after Brian's death. And I don't think you should tell them. Now, my life is my own and I have the right to live it as I decide."

"Now ya'll know I'm going to take good care of her," TJ said. "She's like a sister to me. She'll do just fine, I promise."

Once Julie and TJ got back to the house, Julie had decided to just donate everything to a local homeless shelter and take just her personal things. A fresh start with all new things. TJ had offered the guest house for as long as she wanted to stay, and it was fully furnished. The next day, TJ called a mover to pick up the boxes the two of them were packing up, and to take Julie's car back to Raleigh. Julie went to the law office to tell Bernie of her decision. Ms. Parker expressed her condolences and actually gave her a hug. She led her right into Bernie's office. He stood immediately and gave her a hug.

"I'm so sorry you won't be staying. I had such great plans for you. You're going to be a terrific lawyer, you know? But I understand. You just call me any time day or night if I can do anything for you ever. I'll have Ms. Parker pack up your things and we'll get them to you when you're settled."

Julie was overwhelmed with the support from everyone in the office. They all came over to tell her how much they would be missing her. She left as quickly as she could. The tears were welling up in her eyes and her throat was so tight she could barely speak. When she finally closed the door to her car, she found herself crying. She realized the affection and the respect she had for Bernie and all that he had taught her.

When Julie returned to the house, TJ was taping up the final boxes. "I threw your clothes on the bed with suitcases so you can get them packed up. The landlady is going to let the movers in and the furniture is being picked up later tomorrow afternoon. I think we should go stay at a hotel near the airport so we won't have to drive far tomorrow, don't you think?"

"TJ, I want to tell Alex about the baby. I think we should leave around four in the morning. That will put us in Los Angeles around six. I'll go up to the house and knock on the door. I think he should know before we leave."

"Darlin', have you lost your mind? You can't be knocking on someone's door that early in the morning and just say 'Hey, ya'll are going to be a daddy.'"

"But I want him to know. I'm still going to leave, but if he ever finds out, he'll never forgive me for not telling him. How could I live with myself?"

"Our plane leaves at noon tomorrow. I still think we should leave for Los Angeles tonight and go to a hotel. That way you will be rested before the flight."

"No. No hotel. Let's just stay here for the night and leave early. I know what I'm doing, I promise."

"Well, all right then. We'll do it your way. But I don't have a good feelin' about this. I'm going to pick us up some food. I cleaned out the fridge and I'm hungry. What are you in the mood for?"

"I'm too nauseated to eat. You go and get whatever sounds good to you. I might have a bite or two later. But I just can't think about food right now."

As they walked to the door, Julie spotted Mrs. Rosenthal walking up the walkway.

"Hello Julie," she said as she walked up to the door. "May I come in?"

"Of course. Please come in. This is my best friend TJ. She's been helping me pack and get everything ready to go. How've you been?"

"It's lovely to meet you, TJ. We just love our Julie."

"It's wonderful to meet you too. Julie's told me such lovely things about you and Mr. Bernie."

"Julie, I wanted to come say my goodbyes. This small box arrived for you at the office after you left today and Bernie asked me to deliver it to you. You know we will miss you." Mrs. Rosenthal took Julie's hands firmly and looked her in the eyes. She stared for a couple of minutes and smiled. "It's a girl you know."

"How did you know?"

"I told you before. I'm never wrong about these things. I'm just sorry things didn't end up the way I wished them to go. Well ladies, I must be on my way. It was wonderful meeting you, TJ. And you let us know if we can ever do anything for you. Take care of yourself, Julie."

Julie closed the door behind Mrs. Rosenthal. She stood there with the small box in her hands in shock. How could she have known about the baby? She had only told her mother and TJ.

"Well, aren't you going to open the box or do I have to open it for you?"

"Oh, sure." Julie walked up to the dining room table and placed the box on top as she carefully unwrapped it. When she tore away the packaging, she lifted the tissue paper covered contents, and unwrapped that. "It's a music box," she said as she stared at it. She placed it on the table and opened the lid. It began to play, "Can't Smile Without You."

"It's from Alex. We sang along to that with Barry Manilow during the concert."

Julie's eyes began to fill up and tears streamed down her face. She held it close to her heart.

"That's so beautiful," said TJ. "You should put that in the suitcase. Look, there's something in it."

Julie placed her hand inside and pulled out a photo of the two of them. It was the one that was taken when they arrived at the concert. He had placed it inside for her. That made her cry even more.

"Now I'm surer than ever that I should tell him about the baby."

When the alarm went off the next morning, the two of them threw water on their faces and quickly dressed. Julie took one last look around her home and closed the door. Too many bad memories in there. She knew she had made a good decision in leaving everything behind.

They placed the suitcases in the trunk of TJ's rented car. Julie drove. It was strange knowing she was driving across the Coronado Bridge for the last time. It gave her such mixed feelings. But she knew she had to move forward. For her and for the baby.

TJ slept all the way to Los Angeles. It was quiet in the car and it gave Julie time to think about what she was going to say to Alex. So many questions. *'Would he be happy? Would he be mad? Would he ask her to stay?'* As she drove off the freeway off-ramp, TJ finally came around.

"Where are we? Are we there yet? What time is it?"

"We're close. It's just a few miles from here. It's around six-thirty."

Julie finally made a left turn down Alex's street. The sun was just starting to come up. She spotted the house and saw a car in the driveway. She went to the end of the street and parked on the opposite side, and down a couple of houses. She didn't want him to spot the car if he came out just yet.

"Well Darlin', here we are. Are you going in?"

"I don't know that car. I don't know what to do. I don't know who it could be. Let's just sit here for a couple of minutes. I need to think."

"Well," said TJ, "I'm just going to close my eyes again if you don't mind. Just let me know what you decide to do when you're ready. Let's hope the neighbors don't call the police and tell them there are a couple of serial killers sit'n in a car outside their houses."

Julie sat and watched the door. She watched and watched, undecided as to what to do. Still unsure if she should tell him, she had just made up her mind she was going in. Then, the front door opened, and out walked a beautiful red head. She opened the car that sat in the driveway and got in. Suddenly, the front door opened again. Out came Alex in his robe. He ran barefooted toward the car. The woman opened the window and he handed her a brief case. He stuck his head in the window and kissed her on the forehead. The car backed out of the driveway and he went back inside.

"Did you see that?" she asked TJ.

"Oh Sugah', he's moved on. I told you this was a bad idea. Now let's go. You don't owe him anything. He sure didn't take long, huh? Typical man. That's probably why he sent you the picture. He didn't want it around now that he has a new lady in his life. Now let's go get some breakfast at the airport. We can drop off my car at the rental place and get some grub. "

Julie sat there in shock for a few minutes. She felt as if someone had just stuck their hand in her chest and ripped out her heart. Tears poured down her cheeks. *How could she have been so wrong about him?* She believed he truly loved her just like he'd said. But she'd seen it with her own eyes. He had someone new in his life. And why shouldn't he? She had chosen to go back to her husband. She was angry and hurt all at once. TJ was right. She was going to get on that plane and never look back. She was going to make a new life for herself and her baby in Raleigh. She was going, determined to make a start fresh and try to forget everything about this last year of her life. Her new life would be on her own terms.

As she put the car in gear, Julie felt something inside of her quiver.

"TJ, I think the baby just moved. I just felt it kick. Put your hand here."

Julie took TJ's hand and placed it on her stomach. The baby kicked again and they both smiled.

"Jesus take the wheel! See ya'll, even the baby wants to get the hell out of here. Let's go!"

Chapter 21

The plane finally touched down in San Diego thirty minutes ahead of schedule. Julie was so glad to get off, she practically ran everyone ahead of her down trying to get out. She went straight to the car rental company to pick up her vehicle. Figuring she still knew her way around, she didn't ask directions. But when she went to drive out of the airport, she was amazed at how much the city had grown in the time she'd been gone. She hadn't ever been back. Her parents always went to visit her in Raleigh. They had gone often before her father died. Her mom had moved to Raleigh to live with her shortly after that. She enjoyed having her around, and was glad she'd been there to help raise the baby.

Julie had made reservations at the Hotel Del Coronado. She remembered it fondly and had always wanted to stay there. As she crossed the bridge, she could see how much the island had grown as well. There was so much more commerce than when she lived there.

As she drove down Orange Avenue, she passed the park on her left side. That was where she was to go tomorrow to see if Alex had kept his end of their promise. It had been a lovely affair, and she'd never forgotten him. He'd become quite famous. His name often appeared across the credits of many television shows as the writer, as well as some movies and documentaries. She knew he'd won many Emmys and writing awards and had secretly been very proud of him. Something inside told her he wouldn't show. He'd probably married that red head and they probably had a litter of kids. He always told her he wanted a large family.

When she pulled up to the front of the hotel, she felt quite important. Two valets came right away. One took the suitcase out of the trunk, and the other checked her into her room right there at curbside. He gave her the ticket for the car, and a room key that he made right on the spot. A bellman came and escorted her to her room. The old elevator was still there, but it wasn't in use. The hotel hadn't changed much. It still had the old-world charm. The new elevator had been decorated to look as if it was from the same period as the rest of the lobby.

When they arrived at the top floor, he led her down the hall to a room with a balcony that overlooked the ocean. Julie gave him a tip and closed the door. Right away, she walked outside. She took a deep breath. She'd been to the ocean in North Carolina in Wilmington. She'd even vacationed there. But there was something about the Pacific Ocean she'd never gotten out of her blood. The smell of the air and the water filled her lungs. She looked at the beach where she and Alex had first danced. Where she'd first seen him for the charming man she'd always thought he was.

She decided to change into more comfortable clothes and go down to the beach for a walk. Stopping at the bar to get a drink, she made her way toward the edge of the water. She walked and walked until she was so far, the hotel looked small. As she made her way back, she realized the sun was setting. The magic time of her first date with Alex. She stood and watched it until the very rim was under the horizon. How would she ever sleep? The anticipation was enough to take her breath away. After ordering room service, she laid in bed listening to the sound of the waves until she fell asleep late into the night.

In the morning, she took her clothes out of the closet. She brought a soft pink pleated, off the shoulder dress. She decided to take a long bubble bath in the large sunken tub, a luxury she hardly ever took advantage of at home. She had built a new home five years ago, but was always so busy and in such a hurry she never had time to enjoy it.

As she got dressed, she had to stop and take deep breaths. She was afraid she'd hyperventilate and never make it to the park. Finally, the time neared. Walking through the lobby of the hotel, she fumbled through her purse for the car ticked and handed it to the valet.

When finally on her way, she kept looking in the mirror at herself. Twenty years had gone by. She wondered if he would still be attracted to her. She was excited, nervous, and wanted to throw up all at the same time. *This is so stupid. He's not going to show up I just know it. I'm just a silly old crazy romantic fool.*

Julie pulled up by the park and parked her car right where she used to years ago. Taking one last look at herself and brushing her hair, she got out of the car and looked around. She didn't see anyone near the table by the tree. As she approached, she took a look around and noticed how much the trees had grown, and that the fountain was gone. Walking toward the table they used to meet at, she glanced at her watch. It was time, but no one was there. Suddenly, from a distance, she could hear loud music playing. It was getting closer by the second. She turned and saw a light blue convertible pull up to the curb. Blasting from inside was the Barry Manilow song that her music box played, 'Can't Smile Without You.' She couldn't believe her eyes. He was here! The car stopped, and out popped a sandy-haired man in a navy blue shirt and white slacks. She stood dead in her shoes not able to move. As he approached, her heart began to pound so hard in her chest she could hear it. As he made his way closer, she could see that dimple and that same irresistible smile. When he was finally standing in front of her, he raised his hands. In his right hand was a small white bag.

"I brought doughnut holes!"

Julie began to laugh. Laughing and crying at the same time, she ran up to him and put her arms around his neck. He smelled the same. He felt the same. They stood holding one another for a long time.

"I didn't think you'd come," he said, looking at her. She could see his bottom lip quivering. He looked nervous and excited. "You look terrific!"

"So do you. You haven't changed a bit. Come, sit. Tell me what I've missed."

Alex took Julie's hand and led her to the table. The touch of his hand brought Julie back as if no time had passed. Her hand still felt as it belonged in his. The same electrical feeling ran through her fingers as if she never wanted to let it go.

As they got close, he looked at the big tree that shaded them so many years ago.

"Look, our initials are still there. A little higher though. This thing has grown at least three feet."

They sat across from one other and held hands. They couldn't stop looking into each other's eyes. Time had passed, but that magic feeling between them was the same. They talked endlessly for at least an hour. Time seemed to fly by. They laughed and reminisced, and talked about their jobs. Julie told Alex about her job as the district attorney in Raleigh. He asked about TJ and "Jack Danger, The Tire King." She told him all about their five boys. Alex mentioned to her some of his accomplishments in the television and movie industry, and she confessed she'd been keeping track of them through the media. Then, the moment came. The moment for the serious questions.

"Well, are you still married to Brian?" Julie noticed Alex swallowing hard after he asked.

"No, Brian was killed in an accident shortly after you left for Los Angeles. Are you married?" She waited for the response she thought she didn't want to hear.

"No, never married. No one was ever you. Why didn't you come and tell me about Brian? I always wondered if you'd just show up one day at my door and tell me that you were free. Free so we could be together."

"I did go to your door. I wanted to tell you. But as I waited to go inside, I saw a red head come out of your house. Then you ran out to give her something and I saw you kiss her on the forehead. I just assumed you had moved on."

Alex stopped to think for a minute. "Red head? The only red head I know is my sister. She and her husband moved in with me for two months while their house was being remodeled just about the time I came home from Coronado. It must have been my sister. There was never anyone else. Sure, I dated some. But I never even lived with another woman. I always hoped you'd come."

Julie instantly felt the turmoil inside her stomach. She had obviously made a quick judgment call twenty years ago that had been a terrible mistake. Now all this time had passed, and they could have been together. She knew she had to tell him.

"There is something else you should know. I have a daughter. She's nineteen." She looked at his face for a reaction. And she got it.

"Nineteen?" He looked at her puzzled. Julie reached into her pocket, pulled out a picture and handed it to him. He held it and examined it for a long time. But it took less than a minute for him to see the resemblance and put two and two together. The young girl had long sandy blonde hair, and emerald green eyes. She even had his dimple. Alex's eyes began filling up with tears.

"What's her name?" He asked, searching Julie's face for answers.

"Mandy. Her name is Mandy."

www.ingramcontent.com/pod-product-compliance
Lightning Source LLC
Chambersburg PA
CBHW071717140626
46557CB00012B/943